Five Minute Man

A Contemporary Love Story

Covendale Series, Book 1

Abbie Zanders

Five Minute Man

First edition. August, 2014.

Second edition. September 2017.

Copyright © 2017-2018 Abbie Zanders.

Written by Abbie Zanders.

ISBN: 1976321166
ISBN-13: 978-1976321160

Acknowledgements

Amazing cover and series design by Marisa @ www.covermedarling.com

Stock photos from www.depositphotos.com and www.pixabay.com

Professional editing by Kris at C&D Editing services (cdediting.weebly.com/) who has a much keener grasp of grammar and tense than me.

… and THANK YOU to all of *you* for selecting this book. You didn't have to, but you did.

Before You Begin

Five Minute Man was originally published in August 2014 – my first self-published title! Three years and thirty books later, I'm still awed by the whole author thing and the opportunity to live my dream.

I like to think that I've learned a few things along the way, and the book you're reading now shows the results of that. This edition has been updated, professionally edited, and re-covered. It still has plenty of humor and snark, as well as sexy times and explicit language, so if those things offend you, this probably isn't the book for you.

Still with me? Awesome. Five Minute Man is the first book in my Covendale Series, which will consist of four books when all is said and done. If you like what you read, feel free to check my other titles and click the link at the back of this book to sign up for my newsletter, receive a free ebook, and get a chance each month to win a $25 gift card, just for being your snarky, alpha-male loving self.

Chapter One

Holly McTierney snorted in laughter as she reread the passage one more time. This time, she was careful to swallow her hazelnut flavored coffee first. The stuff had burned like a bitch when it came out her nose.

A five-minute orgasm, achieved in an elevator, for God's sake? *Five minutes?*

Max, her big Siberian mix, looked up at her with those freaky black-rimmed eyes, one brown and one pale blue, from his super-sized fluffy doggie bed over by the radiator.

Holly drew in a deep breath and wiped the tears from her eyes, dog-earing the page and setting the paperback down onto the round, black walnut table that fit so perfectly in the bow-windowed breakfast nook.

Where did authors come up with this stuff? Talk about your urban fantasy! It took her three times that long to achieve satisfaction, and that was using Vinny, her triple-threat Vibonator with port and starboard attachments. As if a man could actually manage something like that with nothing but his penis!

The really sad part was, this particular piece of sci-fi was on the bestseller's list of erotic fiction, while her latest collection of drafts was still sitting on the editor's desk somewhere.

A five-minute orgasm, she thought to herself as she chuckled. *As if.*

It shouldn't have been as funny as it was, especially since Holly was a bona fide published author of romantic fiction herself. But even she had to draw the line somewhere. Soul mates, love at first sight, bad boy alpha males with hearts of gold—yeah, she had tapped those tropey wells with the best of them, but this? *Dr. Who* was more believable.

After rinsing out her mug at the double-basin, stainless-steel sink, she put it into the stylish drying rack atop her custom granite countertop. Holly's kitchen was her Valhalla, the center of her universe, and as such, it claimed top priority when she had a few extra funds after bills, gas, and groceries. So what if the rest of the tiny cottage looked like shit? She spent most of her time in here, anyway. And once she sold a few more books, she would be able to fix the rest up, too.

If she sold more books. An author was only as good as her sale numbers, and staying afloat in a saturated market was getting harder every day. That was one of the reasons she supplemented her meager income with occasional literary quickies on the side.

It wasn't that she didn't like writing freelance for a couple of popular romance magazines; she did. Those short stories paid the essential bills and put food on the table, even if there wasn't a whole lot left over for other things. However, it was selling her books that gave her the biggest sense of satisfaction. Each completed piece was like a much-loved child, and seeing one go out into the world and be successful was every parent's dream.

She hadn't struck it rich—yet. Getting a book out there took time and money. Cover art, editing, advertising—none of that stuff was free. There were plenty of times when she'd had to resort to mac-in-a-box, and Max had to make do with the cheaper, store brand dog food during particularly lean weeks. Overall, though, they were doing okay.

It would all be worth it someday, she hoped. With hundreds of thousands of new books flooding the market every year, becoming the next Katie MacAlister or Alexandra Ivy wasn't going to be easy.

Holly sighed. That was enough lollygagging. Time to bite the first bullet. Forty-five minutes of morning exercises to boost her metabolism. It was a necessary evil so she didn't feel quite as guilty about spending the next several hours on her ass, drinking coffee with way too much cream—a staple for aspiring authors everywhere—and pounding out another desperate attempt at literary success. There just wasn't a whole lot of physical effort involved in crafting a fantasy. If writing burned calories like Zumba, she would be a waif-thin supermodel.

Max yawned as she reached down to pet him before heading toward the guest room, where she had set up her makeshift fitness room. The equipment had been acquired courtesy of local garage sales; pieces that, after a few initial uses, had become dust-gathering, space-consuming, ergonomic clothes racks. God bless those lacking the willpower to stick to their New Year's resolutions!

This room was next on her list to fix up. The old hardwood floors, which were badly in need of a sanding and refinishing, were bare except for the couple of interlocking flex flooring squares she had picked up on sale to preserve her aging joints. The dingy, yellowed walls screamed for some patching compound and a fresh coat of paint.

In her mind, she pictured gleaming white walls, motivational posters, some big mirrors, and maybe a small, mounted flat-screen in the corner. Having an inviting, attractive space to work out might make it easier to exercise. Maybe.

Abs first. She docked her iPhone and let the heart-pounding heavy metal soak into her skin as she kneeled on the circular torture device and swung her ass left and right to the beat. Then it was a twenty-minute walk and jog on the treadmill to get her heart rate up. The chaser was fifteen minutes of strength/cardio circuits of thirty to sixty seconds each—push-ups, jumping jacks, squats, butt-kicks, planks, mountain climbers, wall sits, and calf-raises.

Holly hated all of it with a red-hot burning passion, but she forced herself to do it, anyway. She absolutely refused to go up to the next jean size. Big butts might work for some high-profile celebrities, but Holly doubted she would experience similar results.

Sweaty and annoyed that she hadn't been blessed with a tall, lithe figure, she chugged sixteen ounces of *eau de tap*, plopped her five-foot-two, chubby butt down, and got to work.

Chapter Two

While waiting for the server to take their order, Holly told her friend Liz about the "five-minute man," as she had dubbed him in her own mind. They were at their weekly dinner—Holly's only consistent, voluntary socialization. Liz didn't find it nearly as funny as she had.

"You don't actually believe that kind of stuff is possible, do you?" Holly accused when she saw that faraway, dreamy look Liz sometimes got in her eye when they talked about some of Holly's storylines. Liz was the best sounding board *ever*.

Liz twirled the stem of her wineglass between perfectly manicured, blood-red nails while she considered her answer. One thing about Liz: she was one of the few people Holly knew who really cared about whatever came out of her own mouth. If she said it, she meant it. The fact that she wasn't saying anything now spoke volumes.

"Jeez," Holly murmured when the response was taking longer than it should have. She took a sip of her unsweetened tea, scowling as the tip of the decorative lemon slice pushed up her left nostril. "Have *you* ever had one?"

"No," Liz finally answered. Like the good friend she was, she snatched the lemon from Holly's glass and relegated the offending slice to time-out on the bread plate, which remained empty for them both, given the insidious evil of carbs after six p.m. Liz's unsweetened red wine didn't count since it was listed as a nightly staple on her latest "sugar equals Satan" diet, which was yet another reason Holly continued to see Liz on a regular basis—she was no natural Skinny-Minnie, either. "But I'd like to think it is possible. That there is some man out there capable of making me feel that way, pushing all the right buttons inside and out. I would think, with all the steamy stuff you write in your stories, that you'd believe in something like that, too."

Holly scoffed. "That right there is exactly *why* I write those stories. Because if I didn't, there'd be no sex worth talking about in my life at all."

Liz giggled and covered her mouth.

Holly closed her eyes and let the blush wash over her. "Our waiter is right behind me, isn't he?" Not just any waiter, either, but a totally hot, college-age cutie with big brown eyes and an ass they had both been discreetly ogling all night.

Liz nodded.

"Is he smiling or beating feet with a horrified look on his face?"

Liz's eyes, the only part of her face not covered by her hand, flicked over Holly's shoulder. "He's definitely smiling." The words came out slightly muffled.

Holly exhaled. Today was just not her day.

She took a deep, fortifying breath and addressed the young stud. "I won't be having dinner, after all," she said wryly. "Turns out that the foot in my mouth is actually pretty filling."

Their waiter, whose name tag read *Brandon*, – gave her a hundred-watt smile that probably got into more coed panties than *Stayfree*. He leaned a bit closer, lowering his voice. "For what it's worth, I think you're pretty hot for an older woman."

Holly hid her mortification behind a polished smile she had perfected around age eleven when puberty took a noticeable hold. "I'm flattered, Brandon," she said, lowering her voice as he had his. "With charm like that, you're going to be chasing them away someday. You know, when you're old enough to shave."

Liz turned away, hiding her laughter.

After a brief moment of widened eyes, Brandon laughed, too. "You're all right. And just for the record"—he leaned down farther and winked—"I use my dad's electric shaver twice a week now."

Holly couldn't help it. She laughed. The kid

was just too damn cute for his own good.

Two hours later, while clearing away the remains of grilled chicken and veggie entrees, Brandon picked up the best cash tip he'd had all month.

Chapter Three

Adam looked up when his nephew came in from work, chuckling. Brandon was a good kid. Not only was he on his way to graduating summa cum laude with a degree in architectural engineering, but he was holding down a steady job, too. Living with Adam saved him the expense of a college dorm room or an overpriced off-campus apartment, and Adam liked having him around.

"Good night, huh?"

"Yeah," Brandon said, collapsing on the couch. "These two ladies left me a fifty-dollar tip on a thirty-dollar bill. They were something else."

Adam Grayson sighed inwardly. His young nephew had the same curse his brother had. Namely, he was irresistible to the female sex. No matter where they were, what they were doing, women of all ages were drawn to him. It didn't help that the kid was naturally charming, either. Adam didn't mind so much when the girls were around Brandon's own age, but it annoyed him when older women set their sights on his nephew. He was just a kid, after all, and a good-hearted one at that. The last thing he needed was some cougar getting her claws into him and taking a few bites.

Brandon saw the familiar frown on his uncle's face and guessed his thoughts. "It wasn't like that. They didn't come on to me. They were funny as hell, though."

Relief washed over Adam's face. Only a dozen years older than Brandon, he felt the need to look out for him. "Yeah?"

"Yeah. It was pretty slow tonight, so I overheard a lot of their conversation." He grinned. "They were debating on whether or not it was possible for a man to give a woman an orgasm within five minutes."

Adam choked on his beer. "Say what?"

"You heard me." His nephew snickered. "One of the women said she'd read a book where this guy took a woman in an elevator and gave her a screaming O in under five minutes. She said it was unbelievable, even for erotic fiction. The other woman disagreed."

"Jesus." Was that what women talked about these days? Damn those romance writers. Between them and Disney, they set women's expectations too high for any regular guy to have a decent shot.

"How old were they?" An image of little, blue-haired old ladies debating *Fifty Shades* over Shirley Temples flashed in his mind and gave him a case of the shudders.

"Not very. Thirty, maybe."

Against his will, Adam's interest roused. He was thirty-two and single, wondering if he would ever find a woman he actually wanted to spend some quality time with. Most women his age were already married, and if they weren't ... well, he had found out the hard way on multiple occasions that there was usually a good reason for that. "Thirty?"

"Mmmhmm. Pretty hot, too."

"How hot?" Adam blurted out before he could stop himself.

Brandon pretended to think about it, but if Adam knew his nephew, he had been working on what he would say since the moment he had served the women. In Brandon's opinion, Adam spent far too much time working and not enough playing.

"Well, let's see. One was about five-seven or so, blonde, blue eyes, dressed nice, like she had just come from an office or something. I think her name was Liz."

An image formed in Adam's mind, one of a classically pretty, professional woman.

"Was she the believer or the non-believer?"

"The believer."

Interesting, Adam thought vaguely, but wasn't surprised. She sounded like many of the women he had wined and dined. Pleasant. Attractive.

Predictable.

"What about the other one? She of little faith?"

"Smaller, darker hair with some kind of streaks, I think. I don't remember quite as much about her appearance, but she was really funny."

Adam nodded, practically seeing the wheels turning in Brandon's head. He narrowed his eyes. "Don't even think about it."

Brandon grinned. "I don't know what you're talking about." With an almost believable yawn and a stretch of his young limbs, he said, "Well, I have an early class tomorrow, so I'm going to crash. I'll catch you in the morning."

As Brandon walked off to his room, Adam could have sworn he heard him whistling.

Chapter Four

"Tuesday night is ladies' night," Adam groused a week later, annoyed that he had been had by his conniving nephew. The fact was confirmed when he read the laminated card clearly displayed above the trench of sugar packets on the table. "You set me up."

Brandon's facial expression was just a bit too innocent to be completely believable. "Relax, will you? Just have a couple of drinks, enjoy a nice dinner, and watch the game." Brandon indicated the huge flat-screen mounted on the wall.

Adam narrowed his eyes. He did have a good, unimpeded view of the screen, and the place really wasn't crowded at all, at least not where he was sitting. Most of the action seemed to be at the fancy bar on the other side of the restaurant where drinks were half price. Regardless, his bullshit detector was sounding the alarm loud and clear.

"Do *not* even *think* of sending a woman over to my table, or buying one a drink and saying it came from me."

"I wouldn't dream of it," Brandon lied smoothly.

Adam knew for sure he had been played when two women were seated behind him and Brandon came over to take their drink orders. One was a thirtyish blonde in a stylish gray suit; the other, a petite brunette with cherry colored streaks in her sable hair, dressed more casually in jeans and some kind of loose-fitting top. The blonde had caught his eye as they passed, her pretty baby blues widening with instant interest. The brunette hadn't even glanced his way.

"Hello, ladies," Adam heard Brandon say from behind him. "It's nice to see you again."

"You're just saying that because I forgot my bifocals last time and gave you a fifty instead of a five," one of the women said. Her voice was low and musical, filled with amusement. It was clear she was teasing him.

"You're not wearing your bifocals now," Brandon observed.

"No, but it's Liz's turn to pay tonight, and she's a notorious cheapskate."

Adam discreetly glanced back to see the one called Liz stick her tongue out and flip the brunette the bird at the same time.

Brandon laughed. "I'll keep that in mind. Now,

what can I get you ladies to drink?"

Originally, Adam had planned on eating his meal as quickly as possible so he could get the hell out of there, yet he found himself taking his time. He wasn't in the habit of eavesdropping, but the two behind him were loud enough to be heard without any effort on his part. They really were a hoot and a half.

One of them—Adam thought it was the blonde—was a systems analyst at a software development company. The other, as far as he could tell, was currently a writer, though judging by the way they spoke about people at the office, he guessed they had both worked together at one time.

The analyst seemed nice enough, but it was the writer that piqued his interest. She had a pleasant, soothing voice that was completely at odds with her rather pessimistic and jaundiced views. Oh, she laughed and made jokes—she really was quite funny— but he heard the cynicism underneath.

It was ironic, really. The blonde worked at a software company, yet still believed there was a Prince Charming waiting out there for her. Meanwhile, the brunette wrote romance novels for a living, yet believed the only thing awaiting her was a bunch of frogs.

They didn't talk about five-minute orgasms, but they did have quite a detailed discussion on female sexual aids that he found both shocking and rather fascinating. By the time they ordered their after-dinner coffee, Adam was reeling.

As if romance novels and Disney's false expectations imprinted upon females shortly after birth weren't bad enough, now a man had to compete with thrusting, revolving, life-like vibrators with front and back stimulating attachments? No wonder modern women were so empowered.

His male confidence suffering a mortal blow, he was just about to slide out of the booth and go home to lick his imagined wounds when he heard something that had the blood freezing in his veins.

~ * ~

"Hey, did you catch that guy sitting right behind us when we came in?" Liz asked, lowering her voice slightly.

Holly swirled a piece of broccoli around in the buttery cheese sauce that had pooled beneath the chicken. "No. Why?"

Liz shook her head sadly. "No wonder you can't get any, Holly. The guy was totally hot."

Holly leaned over in interest. "Do tell."

"Around our age. Dark brown hair. Gorgeous icy blue eyes; kind of like Ian Somerhalder's, but more ... I don't know, intense. And not as pretty. A little rough around the edges, if you know what I mean. Clean shaven, but with a sexy shadow around his jaw. Big, broad shoulders; muscular arms and chest. Couldn't see any lower," Liz said, her disappointment evident. "The table was blocking the good stuff."

"Damn. Think he's still here?"

"I doubt it. He was by himself, and we've been here for hours."

Holly sighed deeply. "Figures. If he's really as good-looking as you say, he might have made a good muse. I'm completely stuck on my latest alpha male. I need some inspiration."

"Sorry, I should have said something sooner. Hey, I think that cute waiter kid was talking to him earlier. Maybe he knows who he is. I could ask."

"Nah, don't bother. He already thinks we're nuts, and I have no desire to publicly broadcast my patheticism."

"Is patheticism a real word?"

"It is now. I'm an author. I can do that." Holly slid out of the booth. "Pay the check while I hit the ladies' room. I'll never make it home without peeing my pants. With my luck, I'll get stuck behind an accident or something and wet myself. Here." Holly dropped a couple of bills onto the table. "Add this to the kid's tip, will you? He's the only one besides you who smiled at me all week."

~ * ~

Adam sat back in the corner of his booth seat as the petite brunette walked by. Again, she didn't even look his way. He wasn't sure if he was relieved or disappointed. Despite that, he couldn't help appreciating the sweet curve of her backside, or the way her hair hung in loose, natural waves halfway down her back.

"Brandon," he heard the other woman whisper from behind him. For once, Adam was profoundly grateful for his acute auditory senses.

"Yes, ma'am?"

"Gah, do you have to call me ma'am? I'm not *that* old, you know. Anyway, do you happen to know the guy who was sitting behind us when we came in? You were talking to him before."

"Yeah, he's my uncle."

Adam cursed under his breath and considered changing the locks to his house before Brandon finished his shift. Emergency locksmith service was expensive, but it would be worth it.

"Does he live around here?"

"He does."

Adam pulled out his phone and started googling local locksmiths.

"Is he married?"

"No."

Adam scrolled through his choices.

"Do you see him often?"

"Yes."

"Could you …? I mean, would you give him this?"

Adam paused, his curiosity getting the better of

him for a brief moment. What was she giving him? A card? A number?

"Will you be there?"

Not a card or a number then. An event of some sort?

"Yes."

"Then I will definitely pass this along."

Adam stared at his phone, his finger poised over the call icon. Shit, if he called the locksmith now, the woman would hear his voice and realize he was still here. He would just have to wait until he got outside.

When Brandon walked away to ring up their check, Adam left enough to cover his bill and tip on the table before he slipped quietly out of the booth, heading for the exit. This evening had been entertaining, but now he felt the urgent need to flee. He did not want to be sitting there when the women left. The blonde might try to talk to him, maybe ask him out, and he would panic. He never knew what to say when that happened. He didn't want to be rude, but he simply didn't like when a woman took the initiative. Yeah, he knew it wasn't politically correct, but he was an old-fashioned kind of guy. Flirting was okay; that was how he knew a woman was interested. If there was going to be any asking, though, he wanted to be the one doing it.

Keeping his eyes focused on the *Exit* sign, he rounded the corner and felt an instant impact from his chest down. He looked down just in time to see the little brunette falling backward.

"Ah, fucking-A," she murmured before she seemed able to help herself, wincing as she started to pull herself up.

The words were so shocking coming out of that pretty little mouth that, for a moment, Adam was too stunned to say anything. By the time he held out his hand and opened his mouth to apologize, she was already back on her feet.

"Sorry about that," she said. Her voice was back to being low-pitched and musical, but her eyes were calling him all sorts of nasty names.

"Totally my fault," he managed, his throat suddenly dry. Hell, she was cute. Big green eyes, pert little nose, little or no makeup. Naturally pretty. "Are you hurt?" He reached out to steady her, but she stepped back in a clear message.

"No, just my pride. And my ass."

She zipped around him, her cheeks a lovely shade of rose, not looking back and not slowing her pace until she dropped into the booth across from her friend. Then she put her elbows on the table and covered her face with both hands.

~ * ~

"Tell me you did not just have hot bathroom wall sex," Liz said with equal parts worry and hope, eyeing her friend's bright red face and look of total mortification.

"No," Holly mumbled from beneath her hands. "I was zoning out and just face-planted a guy's chest."

"That doesn't sound so bad. Was he good-looking?"

"Yes," Holly moaned. "Insanely. At least from my view on the floor."

Liz covered her mouth with her hand to hide her grin. "Oh, Holly, you didn't."

"Yeah," Holly replied with a rueful grin. "Princess Grace strikes again. The guy was so freaking hard I bounced right off his chest and landed on my ass. Then I went all über classy on him and uttered a few colorful expletives."

"Oh, Holly." Liz was doing her best to be sympathetic, but it was kind of difficult when she was trying so hard not to laugh.

Chapter Five

Adam looked at the half-page flyer on pale blue paper taped to the toilet seat and sighed. It was wrinkled and smudged, probably from the last several times he had crumpled it up and thrown it away. First, when he had found it tacked up on the refrigerator. Then, on the TV. The last time, it had been left on the inside of the front door. Brandon must have been pulling it out of the trash. The kid was like a dog with a bone.

Cursing, he ripped it off the toilet lid. He had half a mind to rip the thing into little pieces, drop them into the bowl, and piss on them, leaving them there for Brandon to fish out. Let him try to piece *that* back together. Common sense and a temperamental septic system won out over his irritation, though.

He simply folded the flyer and stuffed it into his pocket instead. He was going to have a talk with his nephew later and explain in a calm and mature manner that he did not need his nephew's not-so-subtle matchmaking attempts.

It wasn't as if Adam wasn't interested in the possibilities, but the thought that the blonde had pushed the flyer at the kid bothered him. He had learned the hard way that the chances of hitting it off with a woman forward enough to do something like that weren't good. He was past the "go out and have a good time anyway" stage. He had been for a long time.

Adam sighed, realizing he would be wasting his breath. When he had been Brandon's age, he wouldn't have understood, either. How could he explain to a twenty-year-old that sex wasn't enough after a while? That what he wanted most was what he was most unlikely to find—a woman who satisfied his mind and heart, as well as his cock. Though, to be fair, the sex would have to be pretty good, too.

No, what Adam was looking for was a woman who could just as easily sit in comfortable silence as hold a decent conversation. One who was intelligent and thoughtful. Independent, yet retained an air of innocence. Someone who could live with his old-fashioned, caveman-like mentality without being a doormat.

Someone who, most likely, didn't exist.

It wasn't as if he hadn't looked. Adam didn't have his brother's movie star looks, but he was a good-looking enough guy and had a decent, well-paying job. He couldn't complain; he'd had more than his share of dates and hookups over the years. While he'd had some good times and met some great women, none of them came close to his ideal.

The blonde at the restaurant seemed nice enough, and she had shown interest. If he did go to this book signing thing, she would probably be amenable to coffee, then dinner, maybe even sex. It would be pleasant. Enjoyable, even. But he already knew that was all it would be, because she just didn't do it for him.

Now that little brunette, she was a different story. She had a voice that stroked him in all the right places, and a husky laugh that made his dick hard and his balls clench. And when she had run all those soft, lush curves into him and looked up at him with those big green eyes, he'd had the sudden urge to throw her over his shoulder and take her out to his truck like the Neanderthal he was.

Even now, he couldn't seem to go five minutes without thinking about her.

Holly, that was what the blonde had called her. Adam wondered if she would be at the book signing, too. Then he decided it didn't matter. He wasn't going.

~ * ~

Holly's fingers flew over the keyboard. The

visions and words in her head were coming so fast it was hard to keep up. Rather than write complete sentences, she just jotted down phrases and words, enough to get the gist and flow before she forgot them. She would come back and fill in the details later.

Three days. Three days of absolute gold and enough imagined fantasies to finish her alpha-male novel and spawn the continuing storyline through a few sequels. All Holly had to do was close her eyes for a moment, picture the guy from the restaurant, and the ideas came to her.

Tall. Broad. Muscular. Too rugged to ever be called pretty. He was the epitome of her perfect alpha, at least in looks. Thank God he hadn't said more than a few words and ruined it all. As it was, he had said just enough for her to hear the deep, baritone rumble that fueled the fantasy. If she changed the length of his hair and imagined that body in different period clothing, he could fit into any genre. She could picture him as a brawny Highlander, a fierce SEAL, or an alpha shifter, just as easily as she could see him as the hero in any of her contemporary romances.

At any given time, Holly had between six and ten stories in various stages of development, encompassing a wide range of subgenres. What she chose to work on depended on her mood of the day, as well as her level of sexual frustration. Since Tuesday night, she had been … *inspired*.

Granted, it had been embarrassing at the time, running into him like that and landing on her butt. But hey, if it got results like this, she might have to start scoping out various places and deliberately staging a few such "accidents."

Or better yet, she could just stalk the restaurant guy. She wouldn't even have to instigate another embarrassing physical encounter. Simply observing from afar would be enough to spawn a few ideas. With his dark hair, pale blue eyes, sculpted features, and hard body, the man was the perfect muse for sweaty, erotic fantasies.

He had to be the guy Liz had spotted in the booth behind them, and boy, she hadn't been exaggerating when she said he was hot. Not in a polished, pretty boy sort of way, though. There was something inherently male about him, something that made all of Holly's girlie parts sit up and shout a great big "hey, howdy."

Smelling of clean male soap and deodorant, a bit of stubble around his strong jaw, and a deep, slightly husky voice that Holly couldn't seem to get out of her mind, he really was the perfect inspiration.

The only bad thing was, Liz seemed interested in him. She hadn't come right out and said so, but she had admitted to pumping the server for info and passing along a flyer for the book signing they were going to in a few days.

Holly sighed and absently petted Max with her

foot beneath the table. If Liz *was* interested, her fantasies would have to stay just that—fantasies. For one thing, no man was worth jeopardizing Liz's friendship. And for another, she didn't stand a chance.

Most men took one look at Liz and started acting like lovesick puppies. They never looked at Holly, not unless Liz shot them down and they were forced to troll elsewhere. It was one of the main reasons Holly never went anywhere with Liz, except to their girls-only weekly dinners.

Liz was her bestie, her BFF, her only true friend, really, but Holly's decided lack of people skills and fragile ego couldn't take the rejection she would inevitably face at Liz's side. Besides, her pride wouldn't permit her to knowingly be someone's second choice.

It was for the best, really. She didn't need the aggravation and disappointment that inevitably accompanied getting her hopes up. For the first time in her life, Holly felt truly at peace. She had her own place and did her own thing. Her life was all about what *she* wanted, what made *her* happy.

Holly once again said her daily prayer of thanks to her late great-aunt, whose bequeathal had allowed her to purchase this little cottage and move out of her hometown for good. Great-Aunt Rose had been the only one who had ever understood Holly's love of books, of reading and writing and getting lost in a really great story. The only one who had ever encouraged her to follow her dream. With the exception of Liz, no one else got it.

Both of her sisters, one older and one younger, were blessed with social skills and thought her preference for spending the day holed up in her room with a book was weird. And both of her brothers, one older and one younger, thought *everything* about her was weird. Her parents … well, they were just disappointed. Disappointed she had hit the big 3-0 and still wasn't married. Still had no kids. Disappointed she had quit her job as a software engineer to write romance novels, of all things. Disappointed she hadn't told them she was moving out of town until after the ink on the mortgage papers was already dry.

It had to be that way, though. If they had known about her plans to buy this place, to move out and start living her life the way she wanted, they would have held an intervention. Deep down, they meant well, but they just didn't, or couldn't, seem to understand her desire to live alone or spend her life doing what she loved. That sort of thing was reserved for the spinster types. Or lesbians.

Not that there was anything wrong with either, but her family, especially her mother, was convinced that a woman could only be truly happy if she had a husband and children of her own.

At the moment, she was neither a spinster nor a proud member of the LGBT community. Despite the lack of male *human* companionship, Holly was still a twig and berries kind of girl. Though, if things kept going the way they were, spinsterhood was looking increasingly likely.

However, she did have Max, who was her saving grace. Old maids had cats or parakeets, not dogs. She reminded herself of this known and scientifically proven fact daily.

It wasn't always easy, but Holly loved her fixer-upper cottage, one of the last remaining outbuildings on what had once been a palatial estate belonging to William Penn, for whom the Commonwealth of Pennsylvania was named.

She loved having the freedom to stay in her PJs all day long if she wanted to. And she loved the fact that what little she had was hers and hers alone, and she didn't have to share with bitchy older siblings, annoying younger ones, or—the worst of all possible creatures—*roommates*.

She'd had enough of *them* to last a lifetime. First at home, sharing a room with her sisters. Then at the state university, where she had been paired with a girl whose biggest college achievement was being selected as a little sister in one of the nastiest frats on campus. Really, if you were into that whole "brotherhood/sisterhood" thing, why not at least go for a sorority? And, of course the coup de grace—her disappointing attempts to find a compatible, mature young adult to share an apartment in town.

If there was one thing Holly had learned about herself over the years, it was that she didn't like having roommates. There was no faster way to dislike a person and ruin what might have been a good friendship than by moving in with someone.

In Holly's experience, the quiet, shy ones turned out to be noisy and annoying, especially when she was trying to do something that required peace and quiet, like reading or writing, the two things Holly loved to do most. The perfectly coiffed Debs were actually pigs behind closed doors, and the steadfast and loyal types often proved untrustworthy in the end, stiffing her for rent and horking her food.

The absolute worst thing about roommates? It wasn't sharing a kitchen or microscopic living room, but a communal bathroom. Holly had yet to find anyone aware of, much less a devout practitioner of, the ass-tag convention. Her last cohabiter actually had the nerve to look at her like she was crazy for having even brought it up. As if getting out of the shower and wanting to know that you could dry your face without having to worry if the same towel had just dried someone's ass was a bad thing!

Honestly. And they thought *she* was the weird one.

Holly sat back and re-read the last few paragraphs, her face flushing and her body heating from the latest in a series of really hot scenes. She decided her alpha muse would just have to remain in her deepest, darkest fantasies, only coming to life on the pages of her stories and her dreams.

Who needed the real thing when she had a writer's imagination and Vinny?

Chapter Six

Sunday dawned clear and bright, a perfect early summer day, ideal for doing a few minor repairs around the house. There were some shingles that had blown loose in the last Nor'easter that Adam needed to secure, the rotting step on the back porch he had to replace, and that leaky faucet in the kitchen he had been trying to find the time to fix for months now.

Unfortunately, he didn't have what he needed on hand. It was a damn good thing that new home improvement center opened up in Covendale. He could drive into town and pick up everything in one trip without having to waste daylight running all over the county for roofing, lumber, and plumbing supplies.

After paying for his purchases, Adam loaded up his truck and breathed in the heavenly scent of grilled beef, which set his stomach rumbling. He decided to grab a bite at Lou's Diner while he was in town. Everyone knew Lou had the best burgers, and chances were, he wouldn't get around to eating again until much later that night.

The place was packed, but that was no surprise. Lou's was a staple in the small, northeast community.

After waiting a couple minutes, Adam was shown to a booth along the window. Foregoing the menu since he knew just what he wanted, he waited for the server to come by for his order as he looked outside. He was mildly surprised when he realized his seat had a perfect view of the bookstore across the parking lot.

Or had he subconsciously ended up exactly where he wanted to be?

~ * ~

"I'm sorry the guy didn't show, Liz," Holly said, clutching her bag of discounted paperbacks and her signed copy of the murder/suspense hardcover. She had hundreds of stories on her e-reader, but sometimes she just wanted to hold a book in her hand, feel the weight of it, smell the pages.

"No biggie," Liz said with a casual shrug. She had a bag, too, but hers was nearly all historical, period type romances. "It was more for your benefit than mine, anyway."

Holly stopped dead in her tracks, turning toward her friend in disbelief. "Excuse me?"

"Yeah, he was hot and everything, but too rough around the edges for me, you know? Definitely more your type than mine."

"I have a type?"

Liz rolled her eyes. "Of course you do. Big, strong, alpha males with a white knight complex."

Holly gaped at her. "Who *wouldn't* want that?"

"Me," Liz said matter-of-factly. "I mean, don't get me wrong; I love to read about them. But in real life? Too intense for me. I prefer Armani to Eddie Bauer. Bruno Magli to Red Wings."

"See a lot of Armani in these parts, do you?" Holly teased.

"No, but I can dream, can't I?"

~ * ~

Adam was halfway through his burger when he saw them. The blonde and the brunette came out of the bookstore, each carrying a bag with the store's logo on it. He watched with mild interest as they walked out into the parking lot together, chatting for a few moments before parting ways.

When they split off in different directions, it was the brunette his eyes instinctively followed. She had a nice walk, a natural sway that was graceful without any attempt to impress.

On the far side of the lot, she stopped by a late

model SUV, one of the smaller compact jobs, and got in. The fact that she had been discreetly scanning the lot and had the foresight to check under the car pleased him. Women couldn't be too careful these days.

A minute later, he caught sight of her chocolate and cherry waves as the dark blue vehicle drove past the diner. Once the taillights were out of sight, Adam sighed and went back to finishing his burger.

On a sudden impulse, he ordered a refill on his cherry Coke and a slice of chocolate cake for dessert.

Thirty minutes later, his heart stuttered a little when he saw the navy Sportage listing off the shoulder of the road. Pulling up behind her, he caught the bob of a dark hair by the front passenger wheel.

Adam put on his flashers and got out to offer his assistance.

~ * ~

Holly poked her head up over the bumper when she heard the crunch of gravel and saw a late-model pickup pulling to a stop behind her vehicle. Then she stopped breathing entirely when the tall, male form eased from the truck. It was him! The guy from the restaurant!

"Hi," he said easily. "Need a hand?"

Given the slight hint of amusement in his eyes,

he recognized her, too. Thankfully, it seemed as if he was too polite to remind her of their previous encounter. It was definitely a plus in her book. And if the flannel hugging his biceps was any indication, the frozen lug nuts on the rim wouldn't be a problem for him. Damn Jiffy Lube and their hydraulic tools, anyway.

~ * ~

The woman released her death grip on the tire iron and stood up to her full, not-so-impressive height. Pushing her curls back from her face, she left a nice dark streak across her sweaty brow.

Adam tried hard to hide his grin.

"Yes, actually," she said on an exhale. "I can't seem to get these nuts off."

"Well, that is a problem," he said, somehow managing to keep a straight face. "Not one I'm personally familiar with, but I'll do my best."

She grinned at him, her cheeks pink with an honest-to-God blush. A little explosion went off in his chest. She had the prettiest smile.

It took him a minute to realize she was holding out the tire iron to him.

"Then I humbly defer to your manly expertise."

It took a few good tugs, but he managed to get the tire off with little trouble. He then turned to ask if she had a spare, only to find her standing behind him with it in her arms. Since it was a full-size spare—another point in her favor—it covered her practically from knee to shoulder.

"I would have gotten that," he said, taking it from her.

She shrugged, then stepped back to let him get on with it. "It's the least I can do."

"I appreciate it," he said, meaning it. In his experience, most women wouldn't have tried to help; they would have been content to sit back and let him do all the work. Not that he would have it any other way, but it was the thought that counted.

He finished changing the tire, then carried the flat to her open trunk. After closing the lid, he removed a blue kerchief from his pocket. Rather than wiping his hands, though, he handed it to her. When she looked at him in confusion, Adam pointed to her forehead.

"You have some grease, right there."

Holly's eyes widened, then her cheeks blushed that lovely shade of rose again. He thought he heard her mutter "shit" under her breath, but it was so softly done he wasn't completely sure.

She took the folded cloth he offered and rubbed vigorously. "Did I get it?"

She had, but Adam couldn't resist. "Not quite. Here, let me." He took the kerchief and made a few gentle strokes across her brow. She stood completely still while she looked at him with those big, green doe eyes. It was all he could do not to lean down and kiss the daylights out of her right then and there. He had never felt the urge to kiss a woman quite so fiercely.

"There," he said, forcing himself to take a step back before he did something stupid. "That ought to do it."

"Thanks," she said softly.

Christ, if she didn't stop looking at him like that, he really *was* going to do something stupid, like crush that sweet little body up against his to see if she was as soft as he thought. This time, though, he would make sure the contact lasted for more than a millisecond.

He pushed those caveman-like thoughts back down and simply said, "You're welcome."

"You know, I bet a hundred cars passed since I pulled over, and you're the only one who stopped to help."

Adam didn't know what to say to that, so he wiped the grease and dirt from his hands and said nothing.

They stood there for a few moments in silence, but it wasn't as awkward as it should have been. For some reason, Adam was reluctant to leave and simply kept wiping at his palm long after the grime was gone, shooting surreptitious glances at the pretty woman as he did so.

Dressed casually again, hair loose, face relaxed and natural, she was even prettier than he remembered. Then she opened her mouth to say something and Adam inwardly cringed.

Crap. Everything had been going so well. He hoped to hell she wasn't going to ask him out and ruin it. Or even worse, try to offer him something in recompense for his effort. She was cute and everything, but …

"Thank you for stopping and helping."

He blinked, waiting for her to say something else. When she didn't, he did a mental fist pump.

"You're welcome."

She smiled at him again, then turned and walked around the front of her vehicle to get in. From where he stood, it didn't look as if she was in any particular hurry to leave, either.

"Hey," he called on a sudden impulse as she placed her hand on the door handle. "What's your name?"

"Holly. Yours?"

Good, she didn't offer her last name. That showed intelligence and caution.

"Adam. Do you like coffee, Holly?"

She hesitated. Adam didn't think he breathed during that time. Then she smiled and nodded. "I like coffee."

Relief flooded through him. Suddenly, he felt as nervous as a kid.

"Would you like to have some? With me? Now?" *Great*. He winced inwardly. *Way to sound overeager, dumbass.*

Her eyes softened around the edges, her smile kind. "No," she said, dashing his hopes. Thankfully, though, her next words restored them. "I have to go home and let my dog out. But how about later, maybe around seven? Ground Zero?"

"Seven's good," he said, pleased with her choice. Ground Zero was a nice, clean, well-lit shop with great coffee and a casual, cozy atmosphere. It was the perfect place for a first date. Not that this was a date; it was more of a pre-date interview. If things went well, they would see. "Shall we meet there?"

Holly nodded. "Sounds good. See you then."

Only after watching her drive away did he finally let out the breath he had been holding. So far, so good, but he refused to get his hopes up just yet. He had been disappointed too many times before. Further analysis would be relegated until later that night.

Chapter Seven

"So, Brandon's your nephew, huh?" Holly asked, sipping her hazelnut cream coffee.

She refused to get her hopes up. So far, Adam was the perfect gentleman. Besides stopping earlier to change her tire, which had earned him quite a few points, he had asked her out for coffee and was fine with meeting there. He had even been waiting in the parking lot when she had arrived five minutes early, and had held the door open for her in an old-fashioned, and appreciated, gesture. Once inside, he had asked her what she wanted, then took care of ordering and paying.

She was glad she had taken extra time with her appearance, choosing form-fitting faded Levi's that made her butt look good, and a soft, forest green sweater that accented her eyes. She was especially glad since he looked so ruggedly handsome in his jeans and white button-down with the collar open at the top and his sleeves folded back to reveal corded forearms.

Sitting across from him now, she was also glad she had chosen the corner booth. The muted lighting accentuated the sun-bleached, caramel highlights in his silky, chestnut hair and made her fingers itch to run through it. Two hands on the cup kept her from doing just that.

"I bet he's a handful."

"He's a good kid," Adam said, sounding honest. "Smart, too. He's going to make one hell of an engineer." The way his eyes softened and his lips curved slightly suggested that Adam was both close to and fond of his nephew.

"You're very proud of him."

"Yeah. It's not his fault he inherited his father's curse."

Holly's eyes sparkled with amusement. "A curse, huh? Is that what you call it?"

He chuckled. It was a deep, low, rumbling sound that sent tingling shivers into some of her more womanly parts. "Yeah. Women throw themselves at him all the time. Who would want that?"

"Who indeed?" she hummed, wondering how Adam handled that same cursed affliction.

If she looked closely, she could definitely see some family resemblance, but where Brandon's features were of the picture-perfect, movie star variety, Adam's were more rugged. His hair was a bit unruly, as if it had been hastily finger-combed as an afterthought. His skin had the sun-kissed look of someone who spent a good deal of time outside. A brief glance downward revealed strong, capable hands and a few calluses.

Of the two, Holly knew which one she preferred.

"What about you? Any nieces or nephews?" he asked, breaking into her mental inspection.

"A few, but they're all still pretty young yet. The oldest is in seventh grade, the youngest, about six months." Thinking of the last time she had seen them—at a family gathering turned intervention— the corners of her mouth curved down slightly.

"You don't like kids?"

"Hmm?" she hummed, her gaze snapping back to his. Clearly, he had been watching close enough to catch the slight frown she hadn't stopped in time. She could add "perceptive" to the mental checklist she was creating in her mind. So far, the plus column had a lot more entries than the minus one, which was still shockingly empty. "Oh, no. I love kids. It's just kind of a sore subject with me."

~ * ~

"Why is that?" Adam asked. Normally, he was not so intrusive right out of the starting gates, but he was determined to find something wrong with her. The sooner, the better, too, because the more time he spent with her, the more he was inclined to possibly overlook some of his prerequisites for ascending to the next level, should it become necessary. Once he started settling, he was in trouble.

Holly scratched a non-existent spec from her coffee mug with the tip of her manicured but practically short nail. It was a few minutes before she glanced up at him with a rueful smile. "I have four siblings—two older and two younger—and each of which is married, actively procreating, and professionally employed."

Adam shrugged, waiting for the innate alarm built into all single males to sound at the reference to marriage and kids, yet it didn't. *Weird.* "So?"

She dropped her eyes again but not before he caught a flash of something raw and vulnerable. "So … I'm thirty, not married, have a dog instead of kids, and work from my home. In my family's eyes, that equates to the bottom of the ninth, down by a boatload, with a full count, and our worst hitter just off an injury is up to bat. In other words, all but hopeless."

The baseball analogy amused him, a not-so-subtle attempt to infuse humor in a subject that was obviously painful for her. Instead of shying away from it, she took it, dressed it up a little, and put it right back out there.

"You paint quite a picture."

She shrugged, but there was no mistaking the stubborn tilt of her chin or the challenge in her eyes.

"There's no use in sugar-coating it. It is what it is." Then she flashed him a grin. "You seem like a nice enough guy, Adam. You should know what you're up against."

Jesus, he liked this woman. "Forewarned is forearmed?"

"Exactly." She beamed, seemingly pleased that he had caught on so quickly. "As innocent as this is, if my family finds out about you, they'll hold a family meeting … after the shock wears off, of course. There's nowhere you'll be able to hide that they won't find you. They'll probably try to bribe you. It won't be pretty."

"I take it you don't go out much." Adam's smile grew.

Holly snorted softly. "Not much, no."

Solitude was something he understood. It was the reason behind it that interested him. Dare he hope that she, like him, was past all the superficial bullshit with the dating scene? Nothing else made sense to him. She was adorable, witty, smart, and didn't take herself too seriously. In other words, she was too good to be true. What was he missing?

"Why not?"

~ * ~

Holly sat back, an enigmatic smile on her face. Adam was so easy to talk to and to be around. She had already broken her first cardinal rule: talking about herself and her family issues. Generally speaking, there was no faster way to end an evening. Yet, he was still there, looking unfazed and even slightly amused. Most guys would have left skid marks within seconds of hearing words like "marriage" and "kids," especially from a woman well on her way to spinsterhood who he had just met over coffee. Granted, it was some really great coffee, but still.

What the hell, she decided. She already liked this guy more than she should have at this point in the game. Best to break out the big guns now and save herself a lot of pain and heartache later. As soon as he found out how she paid her bills, there would be skid marks for sure.

"You seem like a pretty astute kind of guy, Adam."

He inclined his head in acceptance of the compliment.

"What do you think I do for a living?"

One brow raised. God, that was sexy. She had never been able to pull that off, though she had once practiced for several hours with a hand-held mirror and a flashlight in her closet when she was younger.

"Is this a test?" he quipped. "Am I being graded?"

Her lips quirked. "More like a game show, really. Think of it as a chance to win fabulous prizes or go home empty-handed."

"Empty-handed? Really? Most shows have at

least a consolation prize."

"I guess I could spring for one of those day-old scones over there for being a good sport."

"And the fabulous prizes?"

"I'm still working on that part."

He grinned, the look in his eyes suggesting what he would pick for a prize if she asked his opinion. She didn't. Just the fact that he seemed interested was enough for her, no fishing expedition needed.

"Do I get a phone-a-friend? Ask the audience?"

Holly felt her lips quirking again. He was teasing her, and not in a mean or mocking way. She liked it. A lot. "No."

"Oh, well, in that case, let's see." He sat back, crossed his arms, then brought one hand up toward his mouth in a classic thinking pose.

~ * ~

Adam was fairly certain he knew what she did for a living, but this was an opportunity to impress her. Normally, he didn't go for that kind of thing, but he was enjoying himself too much not to play along.

"You seem organized and intelligent. Well-spoken. I'm guessing you went to college?"

She nodded, amused.

"Fairly confident despite your self-mockery. You live alone, which suggests competence and independence. You've already admitted you don't date much, and I don't get the impression you're much of a party girl, so I'm guessing you went for something safe, respectable, and relatively quantifiable, like mathematics or science."

He paused. "No, wait. Something with computers … A programmer or an analyst, perhaps. How am I doing so far?"

Her eyes twinkled, but she said nothing.

He put both arms on the table and leaned forward, looking right into her eyes. "But that's not the real you," he said, his voice softer than before. "You *could* do that, and be very good at it, but you'd hate it. It's not who you are."

Her eyes widened, her lips parting in surprise. Her attention was absolute, focused only on him, and he liked the feeling.

"No, there's too much passion in your eyes. Too much mischief to do anything so tedious. Given the clues you've already provided, it would have to be something more creative than that. Something"—he paused for effect, leaning farther forward and dropping his voice even lower—"not so respectable."

He saw her swallow. The smile still played about her lips, but she was less sure than she had been. A bit of anxiety revealed itself in the tenseness of her shoulders. He had her now.

His voice was barely audible. "You're a Dominatrix, aren't you?"

For a moment, her eyes grew huge. Then she laughed. Not a polite chuckle, either; but a real, hearty, genuine laugh that had her shoulders shaking. It filled his chest with sunlight, making him feel as if he really had just won a great prize.

"Come on." He winked. "You can tell me. What are you hiding beneath that sweater? A leather bustier? Lace corset? Whips? Chains?"

It made her laugh even harder until she had tears coming out of her eyes and she was gasping for breath. He loved a woman who could laugh like that. The fact that he was the reason behind it? Even better.

"Oh, God, Adam," she said when she could speak again, wiping the tears from her eyes. "I can't remember the last time I laughed so hard. Thank you for that."

He grinned back. "So, I'm right, right?"

"Not even close." She chuckled. "I'm a writer." Next to Dominatrix, it sounded pretty tame, which was exactly what he'd had in mind. It didn't take a mind reader to sense that she was worried about telling him what she did.

He snapped his fingers. "Damn. *So* close."

In that moment, his mind snapped a mental picture of her—eyes sparkling, smiling at him, radiant. She was quite possibly the most beautiful woman he had ever seen. His heart even skipped a few beats to emphasize that thought. It shook him a little.

"So, what's so bad about being a writer?" he asked, sipping his coffee, trying to regain his equilibrium.

"Nothing." The laughter faded away and some of the uncertainty re-entered her voice. Adam didn't like it at all. "Unless you write fiction."

"Worked pretty well for J.K. Rowling, didn't it?"

"Yes," she said, drawing out the word. She looked down at her mug, tracing the handle with her index finger. He noticed she did that when she was feeling nervous. "But I don't write about boy wizards."

"What do you write about?" he prodded.

She didn't want to tell him. He could sense it, practically see the battle raging behind those pretty green eyes. Finally, her features went carefully neutral, a self-defense mechanism if he ever saw one.

"Vampires. Shifters. Angels and dragons. Medieval Scottish Highlanders. Navy SEALs." She exhaled, afraid to meet his eyes. "I write romance novels, Adam."

Chapter Eight

There. She had said it. Holly stared hard at the tabletop, braced for his reaction. A laugh, perhaps an awkward cough, followed by either a polite suggestion to call it a night or a poorly veiled offer to help her with some "research."

Seconds ticked by in silence. He didn't say or do anything.

Was he shocked? Stunned into silence because he had thought she seemed like such a nice, intelligent, sensible woman? Or maybe he had been taken aback by the fact that he could have been so wrong.

Holly felt the color creeping up her neck, hating that she still cared so much what other people thought.

No, not other people, she corrected. *Him.* Because, she realized, she really liked this guy, and for whatever reason, his opinion mattered.

Finally, she couldn't stand it anymore and

raised her eyes.

Adam was watching her intently, his face relatively neutral, but his eyes sparkled with ... something. What was that? Interest? Amusement?

~ * ~

Holy shit, he thought. *That look. Those eyes.* Like those of someone already found guilty and awaiting sentence, knowing it was going to be bad yet determined to take it with dignity. She was waiting for his reaction and clearly wasn't expecting it to be good. She didn't strike him as the type of person to care too much what other people thought. Dare he hope that he was different in her eyes? That she might be feeling the same unexplainable spark he was and care about his opinion?

"Do you like it?" he asked.

She blinked, nonplussed. "Like it?"

"Yeah. Do you like writing romance novels?"

"Yes," she admitted warily.

"Does it pay your bills?"

"Yes."

"Then you are among the fortunate minority who enjoy what they do for a living. It's not really work if you love what you do, right?"

"Right," she agreed, but her voice still held a trace of doubt. That hint of vulnerability tweaked something primal inside him, something that appealed to his inner caveman. Without conscious effort, this woman continued to draw him in further and further, and she didn't even know it.

"What about you?" she asked, tossing the ball back into his court.

"I, too, am pretty fortunate. I love what I do."

"And what is that?" she asked, her eyes less doubtful now and sparkling with … mischief? "You're not a Dom, are you? A real-life Christian Grey?"

He chuckled. "More like Ty Pennington." He would be lying if he said the idea of dominating this particular woman in the bedroom didn't hold some appeal. It was an effort to remember they were in a public coffee shop and had just met.

"I renovate old houses. The older, the better. They-don't-make-them-like-they-used-to types. Real stone from local quarries. Huge, hand-hewn beams. Hardwood floors instead of sheets of plywood. Plaster walls instead of drywall …" He paused, giving her a sheepish look when he realized he was running on. "Sorry."

"Don't be," she told him, "I love old houses. So much so, I bought one."

Adam felt another twinge deep inside, like a lock tumbler clicking into place. Had he discovered something else they had in common?

"Yeah?"

"Yeah. A small stone cottage. It was built in the late 1700s, or so they say, to replace the original building, which was destroyed in a fire in the late 1600s. I'm still doing the research on that. It used to be part of a much bigger estate."

"Not the gamekeeper's cottage on the old Penn estate?"

She nodded. "Yep, that's the one. You know of it?"

He laughed. "I do. I was actually hoping no one would buy it and I could talk them down on the price." He shook his head in disbelief. Any moment now, he was going to wake up. "Tell me. What's it like? The inside, I mean."

~ * ~

Is he really interested, or is he just being polite? she wondered.

Holly loved her place. Liz often told her that, when she talked about it, she got this dreamy look on her face. That was usually when Liz admitted to zoning out.

Holly didn't want to bore the man to distraction, but he might as well know up front what he was dealing with. He had handled the "I'm a romance writer" thing better than expected, and he had admitted to a penchant for old houses, as well.

Of course, since he renovated old places for a living, he might be asking out of professional rather than personal interest. Inwardly, she shook her head. It didn't matter. He was interested, and she liked being the focus of his interest, underlying motivation be damned.

"Oh, it's beautiful," she said aloud. "It's been upgraded over the years, of course—wired for electricity and fitted for indoor plumbing—but it's retained its old-world charm. The house needs a lot of work, though. I've been there nearly six months and I've barely made a dent."

An idea formed in her head. So far, this man had managed to ace every question on her mental male potential quiz, which was a first. Plus, she liked him enough to want to see him again. This might be the perfect way to do just that without actually asking him out. Whatever genetic trait predisposed her to alpha male type romance novel writing also prevented her from taking the initiative in situations like this.

"Adam, would you be interested in seeing it? Maybe you could offer some professional advice. I want to keep as much of the original look and feel as possible, and I'm afraid I've just kind of been winging it."

He didn't answer right away. Seconds ticked by in silence, feeling more like minutes, and with each one, Holly's disappointment grew. Things had been going so well. She should have just kept her big mouth shut. Obviously, she had misread the situation. The only thing she could do at this point was backtrack and try to regain some of that easy back-and-forth they'd had going on before she had ruined it by pushing too hard.

"I'm sorry. I shouldn't have asked. I'm sure you're very busy."

"I'd love to."

She blinked, her eyes snapping back up to his.

His expression was unreadable, but his eyes, they were intensely blue, darker than they had been just a little while ago. Those eyes were borderline hypnotic and blatantly powerful. If she wasn't careful, she could easily lose herself in them.

"You would?"

"Absolutely." Those blue eyes continued to bore into her, holding her captive.

He had said yes, which meant she hadn't messed this up *yet*, and maybe, just maybe, he wanted to see her again, too.

"That would be great!" she said, trying desperately to sound like the mature adult woman she was and not some crushing teen.

She mentally ran through her calendar for the week, which was kind of silly, really. The only thing that was ever on her schedule was her weekly girls' night out dinner with Liz on Tuesdays. He didn't need to know that, though. She could let him think she had a very busy, rewarding social calendar.

"What works for you?"

"Pretty much any night is good for me," he said, apparently having fewer self-confidence issues than her. "Except for Wednesdays. I'm in a pick-up league at the YMCA with a couple guys I subcontract with."

It was Sunday evening. Monday was too soon. She would seem too eager. Plus, she wanted a chance to clean the place up before he saw it. Living alone didn't provide a lot of incentive to keep things spick and span. Tuesday and Wednesday were out. If she suggested Friday, it might sound more like a date. He seemed interested, but she didn't want to push her luck.

"Thursday night?" she asked.

She felt the effects of his slow smile all the way down to her toes. "Thursday night it is."

Chapter Nine

As each day passed, Adam was convinced he must have missed something. No woman could be that perfect. Holly was close to his age, well past the silly girl stage, but not too old to have fun. On the quiet side, yet intelligent and funny. Beautiful and sexy with just the right amount of curves. Self-sufficient, but approachable. Willing to ask for, and appreciate, help. Plus, she liked kids, dogs, and historic homes.

That wasn't all. They had sat in the coffee shop and talked for hours, and it had been so *easy*. He even liked the way she said his name. Her voice was pitched just a bit lower than average, and she tended to speak softly, so every time she said it, it sounded like a lover's address.

She had bought the old gamekeeper's cottage, which meant she had excellent taste and they shared a common interest. And … the one thing that stole the breath from his lungs was that she had actually invited him over to her place on the premise of getting his professional opinion. It might have been purely professional, or it might not. Either way, she had managed to ask in a way that his inner caveman wasn't offended.

Of course, there was the fact that she wrote romance novels and was apparently well-versed on vibrators, but he tried not to think about either of those things too much. She certainly seemed down-to-earth, and as far as he could tell, she didn't seem to be holding him to any unrealistic expectations. If anything, she seemed even more cautious than he was.

He rubbed absently at his chest with one hand while he poured another bowl of cereal with the other. Yeah, he must have missed something, because no woman that good would still be available.

"Why not? You are," Brandon asked, breezing into the kitchen.

Adam shot his nephew a look, then nearly groaned when he realized he must have been muttering his thoughts out loud. Maybe that wasn't such a bad thing. Normally, he tried to keep his private thoughts just that, but perhaps he could use the kid as a sounding board. Thanks to his own big mouth, Brandon had the gist of what was going on, anyway.

"What do you know about her?"

Brandon shrugged, snatched the milk, and

poured himself a glass. "Not much. Her full name is Holly Noelle McTierney. Her birthday is December 25th, hence the name. She grew up about fifty miles southeast of here. She writes romance novels, and currently has five books published, available online. She's never been married and has no kids, but she does have a dog, Max, that she rescued about a year ago."

At Adam's gaping stare, Brandon grinned wickedly, adding, "Oh yeah, and she has dinner with her friend every Tuesday at Applebee's, is an excellent tipper, and doesn't believe in the possibility of five-minute orgasms."

"How do you know all this?"

A smirk. "Ever hear of Google?"

"You *googled* her?"

"Well, yeah. I knew you wouldn't do it, and someone's got to have your back, Uncle Adam. Oh, and she has a website and social media pages, too. Based on some of the comments posted out there, it's pretty steamy stuff." He waggled his eyebrows suggestively as he finished off his glass of milk, slung his backpack over his shoulder, and snatched an apple from the bowl on the table. "You might want to check it out."

~ * ~

"Holly?"

At the sound of the deep male voice, Holly

gripped the phone tighter.

"Yes? Adam?"

"Yeah. Listen, about tomorrow …"

Holly braced herself for what would come next. She had been expecting it, but as each day had gone by, she had allowed herself to hope a little more. She had made it all the way to Wednesday, but now he was calling to cancel, she just knew it.

Oh well, she lamented, searching for the positives. At least the cottage got a good, and much-needed, cleaning. The anticipation of seeing him again had done wonders for her creativity. She had finished off that historical she had been stuck on for two months and made significant progress on two or three others.

"Yes?"

"I was thinking maybe I could pick up something to eat on the way, if that's okay with you. I won't have time to grab something after work. Unless you have other dinner plans, that is," he added hastily.

He wasn't canceling? He was offering to bring dinner? She pulled the phone away from her ear and stared at it.

"Holly, are you there?"

"Um, yeah, I'm here," she said, leaning against the counter and bringing the phone back to her ear. Max looked up at her and blinked. "Sorry. That would be great, actually."

"Do you like Chinese?"

"I love Chinese," she admitted.

"Great. Anything I should avoid?"

"I'm not big on seafood."

She thought she heard a sigh of relief. "Me neither. So, I'll see you about six tomorrow?"

"Six is good."

Holly hung up the phone and did a little happy dance right there in the kitchen. "He's still coming, Max! And he's bringing dinner! Chinese food!"

Max's ears perked up in interest. He loved Chinese take-out almost as much as she did.

Chapter Ten

Well, the cottage looked as good as it was going to. The floors had been swept and Swiffered, the area rugs beaten and aired out. The wood was polished, shelves dusted. She didn't have an abundance of furniture, but what she did have was vacuumed and treated to a clean-smelling fabric refresher. Max's toys had been picked up and deposited in the baskets she had in each room, though he was quietly emptying them every time she wasn't looking. A vase of fresh flowers picked from the garden out back sat on the table, and a subtly scented vanilla candle burned in the kitchen, mixing with the aroma of the lemon cream cake she had baked that afternoon. The cottage wouldn't win any featured pages in *House Beautiful*, but it looked neat and cozy, and smelled clean and inviting.

Holly changed her outfit no less than six times before finally deciding on a pair of comfortable yet stylish leggings and an oversized tunic tee that was both slimming and managed to make her look a little taller than she was. The resulting ensemble was casual, yet more suited to company than the pajama pants or ancient but oh-so-comfy faded jeans she normally wore around the house.

With a final spritz of light white musk, her favorite fragrance, she checked her hair one last time. She had opted to leave it down, but tamed it with a thin, flexible hairband that she hoped said: "I like you, but I'm not trying to impress you."

Which was total bullshit, of course.

The sound of a truck making its way up her gravel driveway sent a flutter of butterflies through her stomach.

Max's ears perked up, and he moved to the big picture window, pushing aside the lace curtains with his nose to get a better look. He glanced back at Holly questioningly.

"It's okay," she confirmed, peeking out from the side. "That's Adam."

Accepting this, Max went back to looking out the window.

When the doorbell rang a few seconds later, Holly closed her eyes and counted to three, not wanting to seem too anxious. Then she wiped her sweaty palms on her leggings and opened the door.

"Hi," she said, not having to force or fake her smile.

Adam looked even better than she remembered. Dressed in jeans and a form-fitting black thermal shirt, it was hard not to stare. His dark hair looked damp as if he had recently taken a shower. The scent of male soap and something decidedly warm and musky hit her, and she inhaled deeply, anxious to fill her lungs with it.

"Hi." He grinned back, holding two large bags in his hand.

Max pushed between Holly and the doorframe, sniffing at the food.

"Max, don't be rude," she chastised lightly. She looked back up at Adam. "Don't mind him. He loves Chinese."

~ * ~

Adam grinned and followed her inside. He had every intention of looking around and checking out the interior, but he could not seem to tear his gaze from the stunning view of Holly's backside as she walked in front of him. The long shirt covered it, but clung just enough to whet his appetite and be transfixed by the hypnotic sway of her hips.

"Great place," he said, wishing he had actually looked.

"I think so. How about we put those in the oven to keep warm while I give you the grand tour before it gets too dark?"

"Sounds good."

What smells so good? Was that her, or something else? Whatever it was, it was making his mouth water. Since his cock was rousing with interest, too, he concluded that it was probably not just the delicious-looking cake on the raised glass display plate.

She took the bags from his hand and placed the containers in the oven, bending over and giving him a perfect view of her ass. *Heart-shaped. Firm. Perfect.* He just barely managed to contain his groan before she stood up and faced him again.

"This is Max, by the way. Max, this is Adam, the guy I was telling you about."

Max held up one paw as if to shake.

Amused, Adam went down on one knee and took his paw. "You told him about me?"

"Of course. You wouldn't have gotten in the door otherwise. He's very protective."

As if he understood, the dog smiled, actually *smiled*, at him, revealing some very big, very sharp fangs. Combined with his eyes—one blue, one brown, both outlined in coal black, giving him a demonic appearance—he looked capable of doing some serious damage. Thankfully, he seemed friendly enough.

"Interesting markings."

"Yeah. He freaks some people out. I was going to call him 'Devil Dog,' but he seems to like Max better."

"Understandable," Adam said, though he wasn't sure he understood at all. Then Holly smiled at him and he forgot everything else.

"Well, this is the kitchen. Duh, right?" she said, blushing. "This is the only room I've been able to fix up so far, but doing it right takes money and time."

Adam forced his eyes from Holly and took a look around. What had at one time probably been a dining room was now a cozy breakfast nook with a nice view of the gardens out back. Real, solid wood cabinetry and trim completed the space, the grain gleaming beneath a polished, satiny finish.

"The cabinets have been redone?"

"Yeah," she said proudly. "They had about a hundred coats of varnish on them. It took me a couple weeks and a dozen cans of refinisher, but I got them all stripped, sanded, and re-stained."

He turned incredulous eyes her way. "You did this yourself?"

She bit her lip and nodded. "Yeah."

"You did a great job." Another few checks went into the "pro" column. She obviously had good taste, didn't shy away from difficult tasks, and wasn't afraid to get her hands dirty.

"Thanks," she said, clearly pleased by his praise. "The counters and sink I had done professionally, though."

He nodded. She was intelligent and practical, too. "Smart choice. Laying granite is tricky, and you're better off having a master plumber work on the pipes. Solid copper, I'm guessing?"

Holly nodded. "The plumber said he hadn't

seen anything like them in ages."

Holly then led him through the small cottage, showing him the living area, the small guest room/workout area, and the two bedrooms and a bath upstairs. Then they went outside and walked the grounds.

"How big is the lot?" Adam asked, looking around him.

It was a beautiful piece of land. About an acre of cleared lawn surrounded the stone cottage, secluded but within a reasonable driving distance to town. There was a nice stone patio right off the back of the kitchen. Flowering trees and shrubs dotted the backyard, along with patches of flower gardens. It had a very soothing, pleasant feel. Someone knew what they had been doing when they planned it out. Like the rest of the place, all it needed was a little TLC to be paradise. His hands were itching already.

"About five acres, give or take. The property includes quite a bit of wooded land. I like it, though. I see all kinds of wildlife—deer, foxes, lots of bunnies and squirrels. They like to parade in front of the window and tease Max." She reached down and gave Max a scratch between the ears. "He pretends to be annoyed, but he loves it."

"He doesn't chase after them?"

"He does if they're in the yard, but he never goes beyond the tree line. I found him in the woods when he was just a puppy. He was in pretty bad shape. I think he's afraid. You know, leftover trauma or something."

Christ. She rescues puppies, too? He was half-tempted to check under her shirt for wings. Of course, if the shirt came off, he would probably forget about the wings and concentrate on her breasts. Not overlarge, but big enough to fill his large palms.

Right. Not helping. What were they talking about? Oh yeah. The dog.

"You talk about him like he's a person."

Holly stopped and looked at him. "He is, kind of, but better than most of the people I've met. Present company excluded, of course," she added with a wry grin. "We understand each other, he and I."

Adam acknowledged the compliment with a slight inclination of his head, yet wondered what kind of people she'd had to deal with. She had already alluded to strained relationships with her family, but who else?

He wanted to ask. He wanted to know everything about her. But behind that quick wit and self-confidence, he saw uncertainty, making him afraid to push too hard.

"So, what do you think?" she was saying.

What did he think? He *thought* he wanted to go back in the house and see if she tasted as good as she smelled, and felt as soft as she looked. He *thought* he wanted to forget the house and dinner, and spend the rest of the night burrowing into her sexy little body before something came along and burst his perfect bubble. Because, she couldn't possibly be as perfect as she seemed. If she was, then she might possibly be the woman he had been looking for his entire life.

Instead of saying any of those things and running the risk of scaring her away—he was a bit scared himself—he said, "I think this place is wonderful. With a little bit of effort, it could be perfect. You made a good choice, Holly."

Her smile set off a series of fireworks in his chest. It was all he could do not to pull her into his arms and kiss the daylights out of her right then and there. It was a feeling he was becoming all too accustomed to. That particular urge seemed to hit every time he was in her presence.

"Is that your professional opinion?" she asked, fluttering those thick lashes over those pretty green eyes. It was so natural she probably wasn't even aware she was doing it.

"Yeah." His personal one, too.

"I'm sure you have some really good ideas on how to fix it up."

Shit, yeah, he did, and all of them involved him working closely with her, doing things together. He could just picture her in a pair of old jeans, wearing one of his big flannel shirts, hair pulled back in a ponytail, covered in dust and smiling at him as they restored this place together. They would take lots of breaks, properly christen each room …

He shrugged. "A couple. I'm sure you have a few of your own. You've done great so far."

Another smile, this one setting off more fireworks in his chest *and* his groin. He couldn't remember the last time he had been this hard and hot for a woman.

"We can talk about some of them over dinner. Are you hungry?"

Starving. "Yeah, I could eat."

Chapter Eleven

"I really enjoyed your company tonight, Holly," Adam said several hours later. They had eaten the Chinese food he had brought while talking over ideas and possibilities for a quality redo. Then she had made coffee, and they had shared some kind of lemony dessert that had melted in his mouth.

Like the other night at the coffee shop, time had flown by. It seemed like only minutes earlier when he had pulled into her driveway, filled with both anticipation and doubt. Now they stood on her front porch like two awkward teens.

He knew he had to leave, but he was stalling. Leaving was the very last thing he wanted to do.

"Me, too," she said. "I mean, I enjoyed your company." She gave him a self-conscious smile that damn near curled his toes.

"Can I see you again, Holly?"

She shifted her weight slightly. "Yeah. I'd like that."

Adam might have been sitting on the sidelines for a while, but he had been part of the game long enough to know that she was wondering if he was going to try to kiss her goodnight. He was pretty sure she wanted him to, too. Almost as sure as the fact he wanted nothing more than to do just that … and a whole lot more.

If she had been anyone else, he probably would have. He would have pulled her into his arms, kissed her until she couldn't see straight, then coaxed her back into the house to take care of both of them. But, as much as he ached to do just that, he held back.

Holly was different, and this connection or whatever it was between them had the potential to be a lot more. He didn't want to screw things up before he had a chance to find out.

"I'll call you."

"Sounds good."

He reached down and petted Max. "Goodnight, Max. Take care of Holly. Keep her safe."

Max looked up at him with those freaky devil eyes and *woofed* softly as if he had understood.

"Goodnight, Holly."

"Goodnight, Adam."

Turning around and walking away from her was one of the hardest things he had ever done.

When he got in his truck and drove away, he

saw her watching him in the rearview mirror. She was still standing on the porch, one hand petting Max beside her. Light spilled over from inside, surrounding her in a glowing nimbus. All he could think about was how much she looked like an angel.

~ * ~

Holly watched Adam's taillights fade from view. He hadn't even tried to kiss her!

She closed the door and locked it behind her. What did that mean? He had looked like he *wanted* to kiss her. In fact, for a few minutes there, he looked like he wanted to toss her over the back of the sofa and have his wicked way with her, though that might have been purely wishful thinking on her part.

He hadn't kissed her *or* tossed her over the sofa. He hadn't done *anything*.

Was that a good thing or a bad thing? Had she sent out a bad vibe? Or was he just being a gentleman?

That was the trouble with being a writer—her imagination put in a lot of overtime. There were so many possibilities, and sometimes it was hard to distinguish between what her mind had conjured and what was real, especially when it came to trying to decipher a man's signals.

If this night had been a scene from one of her books, Adam's behavior could have meant several things.

Scenario A, and the most likely: After spending some time with her, Adam had decided anything between them was best kept in the "friend zone," though she had sparked his professional interest.

Scenario B, and her favorite: He was very interested, but he was also the old-fashioned, gentlemanly type who wanted to court her properly. This scenario was particularly appealing because it suggested his interest went beyond the physical and had relationship potential.

Or Scenario C, and her least favorite: Not even the allure of this lovely cottage was enough to keep him around, so he had made his exit with polite grace.

There was one more, remote possibility: He was interested in her, but he didn't think she was interested in him.

That wasn't likely. She couldn't imagine she had given him the wrong impression, not when she liked everything about him. That had to have come through. And he *had* been a complete gentleman all night—bringing dinner, listening politely, and saying thoughtful things. He had even helped clear and wash the dishes!

And he had said he wanted to see her again. Sure, a lot of guys said that without really meaning it, but Adam didn't seem like the type to say he wanted to see her and ask if he could call if he didn't want to and wasn't going to.

How could she write successful romances yet suck at the real thing?

Holly changed into her pajamas, but heading off to bed wasn't on the immediate agenda. She was too wired, too full of ideas.

Throughout the evening, she had been mentally translating his looks, his actions, and his words into scenes she could include in her stories. The more she thought about it, the more she was convinced he really did want her.

His gentlemanly restraint forced her creative imagination to run wild with the possibilities.

Adam was not only hot, intelligent, and interesting, but he really was the perfect muse!

Chapter Twelve

"So …?" Brandon asked, looking up from his physics book when Adam strolled in. "How did it go?"

"Good, I think." It had gone well, hadn't it? She certainly seemed interested, but maybe he had misread the signals.

He wasn't good at this kind of shit. For all he knew, she just wanted him for his professional expertise. Maybe she thought that, by being friendly, he was good for some contractor discounts and free labor. It wouldn't be the first time.

No, some part of him said, quickly rising to her defense. *Holly's not like that.*

"Are you going to see her again?"

"Yeah, probably." Hell, if it was solely up to him, he would hop in his truck and go back right then. But that wasn't smart. There were rules to be followed, and right at the top was: *don't do anything stupid*. He needed time to process this and give it some serious thought. He wasn't a kid anymore, jumping in with both feet without taking a really good look around first.

"When?"

Shit, he didn't know. "Don't you have studying to do?"

"Yeah, but this is way more interesting." Brandon grinned unrepentantly. "So …?"

"So what?" Adam grunted.

"When are you going to see Holly again?"

Adam popped open a beer and sat down in his favorite chair. As annoying as it was, Brandon was much better at this stuff than he was, just like his father. He might as well take advantage of it. "What's acceptable these days?"

"You really like her?"

Did he? That would be a great, big hell yes. He nodded.

Brandon sat back, contemplative. "Then you don't want to wait too long. You want to give her time to think about tonight, but not too much. I'd give it three days, then call her."

Three days? That sounded like a long time. Especially when the weekend loomed around the corner with no plans, other than working around the house. Alone.

Adam made it twenty-four hours. Less than that, really, considering it had been after eleven when he had finally hauled his sorry ass home and it was barely seven p.m. the next day. He hadn't been able to stop thinking about her or playing the "what-if" game. What would have happened if he had kissed her? Would he have been able to stop? Would she have wanted him to?

The moment he heard her soft "hello" over the phone, the words rushed out in a jumble.

"Hi, Holly. It's Adam. Listen, I know it's short notice, but would you be interested in getting together tonight? If you don't have other plans, that is."

~ * ~

Before answering, Holly held the phone in her hand and looked at the tub of chocolate marshmallow ice cream she had just bought and the bag of white popcorn kernels. Yeah, she had plans. The same plans she had every Friday night—order a pizza and veg out with Max, watching movies while ingesting empty carbs in massive quantities as a reward for being good all week. Spending time with Adam would trump that easily.

"What did you have in mind?"

He hesitated as if the question was unexpected. "Maybe dinner in town, a movie at the Cineplex?"

Holly frowned. As much as she wanted to see Adam again, the thought of hitting up an overpriced movie theater filled with noisy teenagers and cell phone addicts on a Friday night was daunting. It would be loud and crowded, neither of which she found appealing.

Making a split-second decision, and taking a tremendous leap of faith, she asked, "What about pizza and Netflix instead?"

"Even better."

"Awesome. Pepperoni, sausage, and extra cheese okay?"

She thought he groaned. "More than. I can pick it up on the way. Can I bring anything else?"

"I don't think so. I have a six-pack in the fridge, popcorn, and ice cream."

"Perfect. See you in an hour?"

"We'll be here."

~ * ~

"I hope you're not partial to your crust," Holly said later as she straightened out the edges of the fluffy blanket and plopped down on the floor, picnic-style. The lights were down, the movie selected, the pizza was hot and fresh, the beer cold, and the miniature, table-top popcorn machine was plugged in and ready to go.

"Why is that?" he asked.

"Max usually calls dibs."

They both looked at the big dog who was currently lying on the blanket between them. Though he appeared to be in the same position as he had been only a few minutes earlier, he had snuck, commando-style, several inches closer to the pizza box. His concentration was absolute, as if he could will the pizza into his paws.

"I think I can share. Does he like popcorn, too?"

"Loves it." That was why Holly had pulled three bowls out of the cupboard instead of two.

She worried for a moment that Adam was put off by the way she treated Max more like a person than a dog, but he seemed more amused than anything else. And he did seem to like Max. She had seen him slip pieces of fortune cookies under the table to him the night before. For his part, Max seemed to have taken to Adam just as quickly.

Chapter Thirteen

The movie was both funny and filled with action, a flick about so-called retired special agents finding themselves back on active duty.

Adam had been a little worried at first when she had suggested Netflix. What if she was really into those tearjerker chic flicks? Not that he wouldn't be willing to sit through one if it meant spending time with Holly, but this was so much better.

Once they'd had their fill of pizza, they paused the movie and made popcorn. When they started it up again, she sat closer to him on the floor, enough that their shoulders touched. Warmth spread through him from the point of contact, sinking deep into his overworked, tired muscles. As entertaining as the movie was, it was difficult to pay attention when all he could think about was how nice it was to have her next to him.

As the final credits rolled across the screen, Adam turned to look at Holly, only to find her already looking at him. Her gaze moved from his eyes down to his lips. He had been able to resist kissing her once, but that same strength fled him now.

He leaned toward her slowly, giving her every opportunity to stop him, to turn away, but she didn't.

His lips brushed hers, tasting of salt and butter. They were so soft. Soft and full, parted slightly in clear invitation.

Adam deepened the kiss, his tongue allowing him a proper taste, and groaned. Needing more, he cupped the back of her head, her hair like silk beneath his fingers, holding her exactly where he needed her to be.

It felt as if liquid heat had been injected into his veins. Every nerve fired to life in a wave that started from where their mouths met and flowed outward from there. In those moments, everything else ceased to exist. There was only Holly. Her taste, her scent, her soft and pliant mouth, and the hesitant, exploring touch of her tongue.

Never before had he been so affected by a mere kiss. Never before had he felt such a sense of rightness, nor a blaze of hunger so hot and fierce that it threatened to turn him to ash where he sat.

When he finally pulled away, he looked into her eyes and saw the same dazed wonder he knew must be mirrored in his own. He wanted to say something, but for the life of him, he couldn't think of a single, coherent thing to say. The only words popping into his mind were "more" and "fuck yes."

Her lips were darkened and slightly swollen from his kiss, her skin was flushed, and her eyes sparkled.

She stared at him, her little pink tongue grazing over her bottom lip, and said, "I think Max has to go out."

It took a moment to translate her words over the rush of roaring blood in his ears, obviously on the express train south where the rest of his blood seemed to be gathering.

He was vaguely aware of Max pushing his way up between them, his paw coming to rest on Holly's arm.

Somewhat shaken, Adam leaned back enough to allow Holly to rise.

What the hell just happened?

~ * ~

Holy earth-moving kisses, Batman!

Holly knew she was moving toward the back door, but it was not by conscious effort. Her feet took care of the left-right-left-right forward motion, her hand automatically reached for and opened the door. She even managed to step out into the cool summer evening and inhale a few deep breaths.

She had read about kisses like that. Had even written about them herself. However, she had never actually experienced one before.

One minute, she and Adam were sitting next to each other; the next, his lips were on hers and she was lost. For a few minutes, everything else ceased to exist, and there was only *Adam* ...

The feel of Adam, all hot, hard, and warm.

The taste of Adam, salty, sweet, and spicy.

The scent of Adam, clean, fresh, and male.

If not for Max's interruption, would they still be kissing? Or would they have progressed to other things? Would Adam's hand have moved to cup something other than the back of her head? Would his skilled mouth have found something besides her lips to stroke and sip?

More importantly, would she have allowed it?

Absolutely.

Holly wrapped her arms around herself and shivered, and not from the gentle breeze. It was completely unlike her to lose control so quickly, especially over a *kiss*.

But, Good Lord, what a kiss!

Holly was a staunch advocate for the five-date rule: no sex until after a minimum of five dates, and they had to be *good* dates that spanned a multitude of venues and activities, not just hanging out at a bar or watching a game. Since she could count the number of men who had actually made it that far on one hand, she didn't have a lot of experience. Of those who *had* made it to the magical fifth date, none had managed to light a fire in her core the way Adam's kiss had just done.

Had it been the same for him? She had been pretty out of it when he had finally broken away, but when she had managed to pry open her eyelids, she thought he had looked every bit as lost in the moment and stunned as she felt.

Her lady parts tingled with a potent combination of hope, lust, and anxiety.

The big question was: what was she going to do about it? Technically, this was only the third time her and Adam were seeing each other. Coffee, dinner and a house tour, pizza and a movie. Was she willing to break her five-date rule? Was she strong enough to go back to kissing—*yes, please!*—and *not* melt into a puddle of desire at his feet?

One thing was for certain, she thought as she impatiently waited for Max to do his business. She sure wasn't going to find any answers out on her porch.

As it turned out, she wasn't going to find any in her living room, either.

Chapter Fourteen

Adam put the last of the throw pillows back on the couch with a little more force than necessary. The television was off, the remnants of their indoor picnic had been gathered, and the immediate area tidied.

He was still reeling from that kiss, though it seemed woefully inadequate to describe what they had shared simply as a kiss. He had kissed women before. This had been different.

He could still taste her on his lips, still feel the way she had softened so readily for him. His thirty-two-year-old body felt eighteen again, hot and hard, and pumped up with primal urges. His heart raced, filled with promises, even as his mind warned him to slow the hell down.

From a fucking *kiss*.

He didn't have to turn around to know that Holly had returned; he could sense her. His cock throbbed in welcome as she hovered in the archway separating the living space from the kitchen area, looking every bit as off-balance as he felt. It was that, the hint of vulnerability, that made up his mind for him.

"I should be going," Adam said huskily. His eyes flicked over her, but he didn't hold her gaze. If he allowed himself to look into her eyes and see the passion burning just below the surface, he couldn't be responsible for his actions. He wanted her with a ferocity that shook him to his core.

Disappointment and confusion flashed in her eyes as Holly accepted the empty popcorn bowls he thrust into her hand. "Okay."

"I had a great time." The words fell so far short of the mark that he winced. It sounded more like an insincere platitude than the heartfelt sentiment it was. The evening had been perfect, exactly what he needed after a long day of busting his ass. *Holly* had been perfect.

How was it that he felt so comfortable, so at peace around her, when he hardly knew her? At least until he had started kissing her. Then the comfort and peace burned up like dry tinder in the sudden flames consuming him from the inside out.

"Me, too."

Was that a reflexive response or a genuine one? It was hard to tell. Her voice gave nothing away, and she was looking down at the bowls in her hands instead of at him so he couldn't see her expressive eyes.

"Thanks for having me." *Shit! That sounded even worse.* Forget eighteen. He had regressed to the awkward banter of a twelve-year-old.

"My pleasure."

She walked him to the door and opened it, keeping her body slightly behind it as if subconsciously putting a barrier between them. Unlike the other night, she made no move to follow him onto the porch.

Adam hesitated. Maybe leaving was a mistake. It wasn't like him to panic like that. Maybe he just needed to take a breath and follow his instincts. She had been right there with him, he was sure of it.

Holly made the decision for him. "Drive safely."

Nodding, he turned and walked to his truck. This time when he looked in the rearview mirror on his way out, he didn't see her watching him go.

Well, shit.

~ * ~

Holly didn't hear from Adam for the rest of the weekend. She tried not to read too much into that, but it was hard not to, especially after the kiss they had shared.

"Kiss" really didn't describe it at all. It was like trying to call the Adirondacks a series of consecutive bumps in the landscape.

Maybe that had just been her. He might have not felt the same rush, the same all-encompassing tingles that had raced through her body demanding *more*. Hell, he might have felt just the opposite.

She didn't think so, though. Right afterward, when she had looked into his eyes, she could have sworn she saw the same awe, the same surprise she had felt.

Although, it might be easier to believe that if he hadn't practically left skid marks on his way out.

The gum-smacking hostess at Applebee's was one they hadn't seen before. Holly decided right off the bat she didn't like the girl, especially when they were told Brandon's section was full and they were seated on the other side of the restaurant.

"Whatever happened to the customer always being right?" Holly muttered.

Liz looked back, narrowing her eyes at the young, ebullient foursome of college-aged girls sitting at Liz and Holly's usual table and shamelessly vying for Brandon's attention. As a matter of fact, nearly all the tables in his section were occupied by young females.

She snorted. "Looks like we've been put out to pasture."

"Whatever," Holly said, feigning disinterest. She had been hoping maybe Brandon would say something about his uncle, but that wasn't likely to happen now. "Next week, maybe we should change things up a little. We can hit up Chili's or Olive

Garden instead."

"Works for me." God bless Liz, she *got* it.

After waiting much longer than usual, they gave their selections to the plump, middle-aged server with the bad dye job.

Liz wasted no time swooping in for the scoop the moment the woman moved away. "So ... What's up with you and the contractor?"

Because Liz was her best friend, and because Holly felt like she was going to implode if she didn't talk to someone, she brought Liz up to speed. Maybe Liz could help her sort things through, because Holly wasn't doing very well on her own. A best friend's biased, semi-objective analysis was just what she needed.

"Back to back evenings, then nothing?" Liz asked, frowning. "What's up with that?"

"You're the one with real-life experience. I was hoping you could tell me."

"Maybe he's afraid things are moving too fast," Liz said thoughtfully. "If you guys hit it off as well as you say you did, he's probably pissing his pants right about now. He might just be giving it a few days, letting things settle until he can make sense of them."

"Maybe," Holly said doubtfully.

"Or ... maybe he's waiting for you to make the next move. He asked you to coffee, you invited him over, then he called and asked you out. Could be your turn."

It sounded reasonable enough when Liz put it that way, but Holly didn't think so. It just didn't feel right.

"You think?"

Liz shrugged. "Hard to say. Some guys love it when the woman makes a move, some guys hate it. What's your read on him?"

"I don't know." Holly wasn't sure that second time really counted as her asking him out, especially since they spent most of the night talking about renovating her cottage. Adam had been the one to suggest and provide dinner, so technically, he was the one who turned it into something more than a professional consult, not that she minded in the least.

"I'm not sure I'd feel comfortable calling him." If he was having doubts, he might see it as pushy.

"Yeah. I got the impression he likes to be the one taking the lead." Liz tapped her fingernails, now a dark blue with silver sparkles, against the table. "You said he has pick-up games at the Y, right? Why not come to my yoga class with me this week? You could accidentally run into him on purpose and see how he reacts."

After briefly considering the idea, Holly nodded. "Sounds like a plan."

Liz had been trying to get her to go for a while now. As much as she eschewed the idea of exercising in public, it would be worth it to see Adam again. She could use his reaction to seeing her as a kind of sign post, hopefully providing direction into the nebulous realm of what-the-heck-is-he-thinking. She could stop all of this non-productive obsessing and guessing, and move on from there.

"Great. We can hit Target"—Liz pronounced it *tar-jhay*—"after dinner tonight and pick up a mat and some flattering yoga pants for you."

Holly frowned. "Why can't I just wear my sweats?"

Liz rolled her eyes and gave Holly a suffering look. "Because we want him to notice your ass."

Chapter Fifteen

Adam's head wasn't in the game. He had let too many guys get by him because he had caught a glimpse of Holly on the way in. She had been in one of the group exercise rooms, looking way too flexible in a tight black number that hugged her curves like a high-performance vehicle on a mountain road. Her hair had been pulled back into a ponytail as she smiled at the young yoga instructor who had been trying to demonstrate a pose that put her cute little ass high in the air and slammed *him* with a wave of heavy lust in the process.

He forced himself to concentrate, stealing the ball and driving down the court. Shoot. Miss again. *Damn.* Well, at least he was consistent. He hadn't made a decent shot all night.

After the game, Adam hovered near the door, hoping to catch another glimpse of Holly. He hadn't called her since leaving her place abruptly on

Friday. Hell, if the dog hadn't intervened, he wouldn't have been able to stop himself. That soul-searing kiss would have turned into some heavy petting, the kissing and fondling of several other areas, and probably hot and sweaty sex right there on her living room floor. *Why* that might have been a bad thing, he was having trouble reasoning out. What he did know was that he didn't want to cock things up by moving too fast.

Had she been disappointed that he had turned tail and run? Or relieved?

"You're off your game tonight," his friend Chuck observed as they gathered their things. "Everything okay?"

Adam shrugged while refilling his water bottle. "Yeah. It happens."

Chuck looked doubtful, then he caught sight of something over Adam's shoulder and grinned. "Never mind. I get it now."

All Adam could think of was that Chuck had spotted Holly in that form-fitting spandex. Chuck couldn't possibly know about him and Holly since he hadn't told anyone, but any guy with a working pair wouldn't fail to notice her. The thought tapped into his inner caveman and released something sharp and ugly. He turned, ready to place himself between Holly and anyone else's line of vision and was immediately sorry he had.

"What's her name again? Ellen? Erin?" Chuck asked quietly when the woman caught sight of

Adam and started making her way over to them.

"Eve," Adam said with little enthusiasm and a whole lot of dread. For one very long night, he'd had to endure just how cute she had thought it was that his name was Adam and her name was Eve, a "sure cosmic sign" that they were fated to be together.

"Right." Chuck laughed. "Uh-oh, she has an apple. Prepare to be tempted."

Adam groaned. Eve really did have an apple in her hand. Not that she needed it. On the surface, the woman was temptation personified. Tall and blonde, with a fuck-me smolder that was so perfect she must have practiced in front of a mirror for hours. Her feminine assets were beautifully displayed, wrapped in workout gear that was more seductive than sporty. Unfortunately, beneath the pretty packaging, the inside wasn't nearly as nice.

It was a lesson Adam had learned the hard way. In a classic case of thinking with his little head instead of his big one, he had made the mistake of taking Eve up on her offer once, and he had regretted it ever since.

Dammit. How could he have forgotten that she taught Zumba Wednesday nights? It was a testament to just how out of it he was. If he hadn't been so distracted with the idea of seeing Holly, he could have slipped out the back like he usually did. Now he was stuck in the doorway, visible to anyone in the corridor. It would be impossible to make a clean getaway without being obvious.

Regardless, it was too late now. Eve had spotted him. *Double damn.*

"Hi, Adam," she purred.

"Hi." He did his best to not look her directly in the eye. Unlike Holly, Eve was almost as tall as he was.

A picture flashed in his mind of Holly tucked into his body, head tilted, her big green eyes looking up into his face. Funny how she seemed to fit perfectly against him despite their height differences.

Eve stepped closer in a clear violation of his personal space. Adam stepped back, his body language speaking for him with a very loud and clear "not interested, please move on" message. Unfortunately, Eve wasn't one to pick up on subtle clues.

"I didn't know you still played here," she chastised lightly.

Shit, busted.

"Sometimes." He wondered how the guys would feel about switching their games to Tuesdays. It was the one night of the week he knew Holly had standing plans with her friend, according to his nephew.

Eve's eyes fixated on a bead of sweat that dripped down his neck, blazing with interest, as it disappeared beneath his tank. She licked her lips. Adam's inner caveman cringed.

"When I called the other night, Brandon said you went to a woman's house. Should I be worried?" She placed her index finger on his bicep and dragged it downward, scraping lightly against his skin. It was a bold move, and one he didn't appreciate.

There had been a time when such a deliberate act might have roused his masculine interest, but no longer. Now it seemed he was stirred by petite brunettes who lived alone and were completely unaware of their own desirability. One petite brunette in particular, who should be passing by any moment. He needed this little unwelcome reunion over, pronto.

"No," he answered without hesitation. Eve didn't have anything to be worried about because he was never going to see her again. The fact that he hadn't returned her calls in the past couple of months should have given her a clue. Unfortunately, as he had already discovered, Eve was the type to overlook those kinds of things.

Along those lines, he made a mental note to have a word with his nephew the minute he got home. Brandon probably thought telling Eve that Adam was out with someone else would deter her, but Brandon didn't know Eve well enough to know the lengths she was willing to go through to get what she wanted. For some unfathomable reason, she had decided she wanted *him*.

"Who is she? Do I know her?"

There was no way in hell he was going to give Eve Holly's name. The last time Eve had seen Adam with someone, the poor woman had received harassing phone calls for a week and had refused to go out with him again, saying he was a nice guy but she didn't want to have to deal with his unstable ex. He hadn't been too disappointed, but it had pissed him off just the same. He wouldn't take that same chance with Holly. What if she decided she didn't want to deal, either?

No, as much as he wanted to remind Eve there was nothing between them and never would be, the crowded corridor was neither the time nor the place to set her straight … again. He knew from experience, and the several polite times he had tried to convince her he wanted nothing more to do with her, that Eve tended not to take rejection well. The last thing he wanted was a scene.

Adam really didn't give a shit what anybody thought, but he didn't want to chance Holly witnessing Eve's theatrics. It was far better to diffuse and redirect now, then handle the heavy stuff later.

"It was business."

"Oh," Eve said, her features changing from stormy to friendly again in an instant. Adam breathed a sigh of relief. "That's different. Why didn't Brandon just say so? Want to go out this weekend? My friend's band is playing downtown."

Adam didn't hesitate. "No." He looked over

Eve's shoulder, scanning the faces. *Shit*. Was that Holly's friend coming toward them?

"Then how about we just go to my place?"

"Sorry, Eve. I have to run."

Adam was not by nature a rude man, but sometimes there just was no choice.

He spun around and made for the door. As much as he wanted to see Holly, he didn't want her anywhere near Eve. He would wait in the parking lot. With any luck, Eve would be gone by the time Holly came out.

~ * ~

Holly ducked out of sight around the corner, thankful for the tall potted plant that hid her from view, wishing it absorbed the sound of voices, as well. She had come out a few minutes earlier to refill her water bottle while Liz chatted—i.e. flirted shamelessly—with the svelte male yoga instructor. She had only just spotted Adam, looking exceptionally hot in his shorts and wife-beater tank, coming out of the gym with his friend.

Muscles and a physique that she had only guessed at up to this point made a lovely display indeed, formed and honed by years of manual labor. Broad shoulders, solid chest, naturally sculpted but not gym-ripped. It was the whipped cream icing on a very delectable Adam cake.

Holly was about to approach him when another

woman beat her to it.

Fighting back an irrational surge of both jealousy and envy—the woman looked like something right out of *Playboy* or *Penthouse* with mile-long legs and a set of double-Ds that defied gravity—Holly had stepped back into the shadows. A quick exit was preferable, but there was no way to accomplish that without being seen. To reach the main doors, she would have to cross right in front of them.

Who was that woman? Judging by the way she leaned close to Adam and was touching him, they were more than casual acquaintances. Holly couldn't see Adam's face, but she could see the woman's. There was no mistaking what was on *her* mind.

"When I called the other night, Brandon said you went to a woman's house. Should I be worried?"

Holly's her ears involuntarily tuned into the dialogue taking place only a few feet away. She turned her back to them and raised her hood, trying to untangle the earbuds she carried in her pocket.

Eavesdropping was not her thing on the best of days, and she was quite sure she didn't want to listen in on this exchange. If she could just get her buds in, she could listen to music until they moved on and pretend that crampy, sick feeling in her stomach was from that last set of locust poses.

"No."

Holly heard Adam's answer clearly. Despite her best attempts, her fingers weren't moving fast enough to get the buds plugged into her phone and into her ears in time.

"Who is she? Do I know her?"

"It was business."

Shit, shit, shit! La-la-la! Stop listening! Goddamn made-in-Taiwan pieces of shit! No matter how carefully she wound them, they always got tangled.

"Oh, that's different. Why didn't he just say so? Want to go out this weekend? My friend's band is playing downtown."

Holly didn't wait to hear his answer. Ensuring her hoodie was in place, she slipped in front of the group of guys coming out of the gym, being extra careful to keep her back to Adam and his … whatever. For once, she was thankful for her lack of height; it would be all but impossible to see her in front of the guys.

She climbed into her Sportage and sent a quick text to Liz. *Good luck with Mr. Flexible. I'm heading out. Call me tomorrow with details.*

Holly took a deep breath and turned the key. At least now she didn't have to wonder anymore why Adam hadn't called her.

In the twenty-minute drive back to her place, Holly refused to think about what she had just seen and heard, forcing herself to concentrate on the road. Once she got home, however, it was a different story.

"He's probably feeling guilty," she told Max later, putting a scoop of special doggy "ice cream" into his dish, then two scoops of the real thing into hers.

She blamed herself, at least partially. She had never bothered to ask if Adam was involved with anyone. She had just assumed otherwise, which was stupid on her part.

"That's why he left like his pants were on fire and hasn't called since. He wasn't supposed to kiss me. Things just got out of hand and he freaked. Caught up in the moment, that's all. Happens all the time, right?"

Holly sat down at the kitchen table and stuffed a big spoonful into her mouth. "And me, thinking all that stupid shit! Me, of all people! I should know better than anyone that that 'finding the right one' crap doesn't happen in the real world. If it did, people wouldn't need to buy my books, now would they?"

Max looked up at her, licking away the last of the treat from his muzzle.

"I know, right?" she said around the spoon, hearing the words her faithful companion was incapable of vocalizing in her mind. "I'm pathetic. Falling for my own drivel."

Holly scraped out the last of the chocolate marshmallow then put her bowl in the dishwasher, along with Max's. "I blame myself. And Liz. All that shit about alpha males and five-minute men pushing the right buttons. What a crock of shit." She added some detergent then slammed the door closed harder than necessary.

Adam *had* pressed quite a few of her buttons. He was good-looking and well-built. Intelligent. And had his own successful business restoring old houses, for crying out loud. Family was obviously important to him since he let his nephew live with him while he went to college, and glowed with pride whenever he talked about him.

Oh, and he could get her lady parts singing with nothing more than that deep voice and a kiss.

Except for the thrum of sexual tension between them, he had been so easy to be around. Holly had felt comfortable enough with him to talk about her family and her career, both things she rarely spoke of with anyone besides Liz. She had even felt safe enough to invite him to her home.

She was an idiot. Why would Adam ever want someone like her when he had that blonde centerfold at his beck and call? Holly was pretty sure that, when Adam was with *her*, they weren't eating pizza on the floor and streaming movies.

Of course she already knew the answer to that question, especially since she had heard the answer from Adam himself. *It was business.* Right. Because she had a centuries-old stone cottage that needed a shitload of restoration and, conveniently enough, that was what he did for a living.

She had been the one who had invited him over and solicited his professional opinion.

Holly let Max out one more time, then locked up the house and headed for the shower. Yeah, it was no wonder Adam was willing to put in a little extra effort to garner her business. He had probably been picturing his retirement fund the whole time she was giving him a tour.

There had been that kiss, though … There had been nothing business-related about *that*. Then again, just because it had tilted her axis didn't mean it had done the same thing for him. The fact that he had bolted right afterward and hadn't called since should have been a great big clue, and tonight's encounter had put the last piece of the puzzle into place.

Holly pulled an old, oversized college jersey over her head, taking comfort in the familiar way the hem touched mid-thigh. Then she brushed her hair and her teeth, taking a good look at herself in the mirror. Tiny lines were starting to become visible around the corners of her eyes and mouth. Though she was far from looking old, she no longer had the dewy glow of youth she once had. There was nothing remarkable about her features. She had the same green eyes and brown hair as the rest of her family, though the dark cherry streaks were a personal indulgence, a symbolic middle-finger to those who decried her creativity and independence.

She was also a realist and had to face facts.

Even on her best hair day, she couldn't compete with the stunning blonde perfection of the Nordic-looking Zumba instructor.

Deciding to forego any attempt at writing—undoubtedly, whatever she came up with would reflect her crappy mood—she crawled into bed.

Max was there a moment later, more than happy to curl up next to her on the other side of her queen-sized bed. He settled down on the pillow with a big sigh and looked at her with his mismatched eyes.

Holly reached out and let her fingers rake through his thick, silky fur. It was no wonder dogs were brought to hospitals and retirement homes. Just the fact that he was there was a comfort. Between Max and Turkey Hill's chocolate marshmallow swirl, Holly could handle just about anything.

Self-pity was not her thing. This was just another bump, another life lesson to remind her why she had chosen to leave her corporate-based career and move out into her own secluded bubble. She just wasn't wired like everyone else, and sometimes, she forgot that.

One night. That was all she would allow for feeling sorry for herself. Tomorrow, she would wake up and get right back into the swing of things, a little smarter than she had been yesterday.

Chapter Sixteen

The phone rang several times until Holly's voicemail picked up with a generic message. Adam looked at the display and confirmed that he had punched in the right digits since there was nothing to identify it as Holly's voicemail—a common but inconvenient safety measure.

Suddenly, he realized he had no idea what to say. As he listened to the computer-generated voice, he ran through and dismissed the first couple things that came to his mind.

Hi, Holly, it's Adam. Sorry I panicked and ran out of your house last Friday.

Hi, Holly, it's Adam. I saw you at the Y tonight and you looked really hot. I couldn't hang around for you, though, because a crazy stalker caught sight of me first.

Hi, Holly, it's Adam. I can't stop thinking about you.

All were true, but probably not the best messages to leave on her voicemail.

The monotoned instructions ended, followed by a muted beep that told him he was out of time.

"Hi, Holly, it's Adam. There's a big expo this weekend over in Dalton. Lots of great ideas for renovating, if you're interested. My number is on the card I left at your place, but just in case …"

Adam hung up after leaving his number and frowned. Where was she, anyway? It was nearly eleven o'clock at night. He didn't feel bad about calling so late; she had confessed to often working into the wee hours of the morning. It was when she wrote some of her best stuff, she had said.

Had she gone out with her friend after the Y? That had been hours ago. Maybe she was in the shower. Or outside with Max. Yeah, that was probably all it was. She would call him back in a few.

After seeing her earlier, he wanted to hear her voice again. Thanks to Eve's untimely arrival, he had missed the opportunity to speak with her in person; she must have slipped out while he was occupied. He would have to make do with hearing her voice over the phone.

He couldn't get her out of his mind. It had been five days—more than enough time to convince him that whatever this thing was between them, he wanted to pursue it. No woman had ever managed to affect him so thoroughly or so quickly, and that had to mean something, right?

He waited until midnight, checking his phone every few minutes, but she didn't call. Maybe she figured it was too late. He had told her that he liked to get an early start. Yeah, she was being considerate. She would call him back tomorrow.

~ * ~

The moment his alarm went off, Adam pulled out his cell and checked again. Nothing, except for one text that had come through somewhere just before dawn: *Thanks, but I can't.*

That was it. No further explanation. No "I'll call you later," or implied invitation, or suggested alternatives. Four words that seemed strangely distant and impersonal from the woman who was anything but.

He tried again Thursday night. Holly had been free last Thursday. Logic suggested she might be again this week. He frowned when her voicemail picked up again.

"Hi, Holly, it's Adam. Got your text. Sorry you can't make it to the expo. Are you interested in grabbing a coffee or something? If you give me a list, I can check out some things for you while I'm there."

Adam ended the call and shook his head. *Way to go, Romeo.* Why didn't he just bite the bullet and ask her out? Instead, he had to hide behind some lame business excuse. Yeah, the expo was cool, but more importantly, it seemed like the perfect opportunity to spend the day with Holly. A nice, long car ride, walking around the half-million square foot indoor arena, maybe impressing her a little bit with his knowledge. Then he would casually suggest dinner, and when he took her home, she would invite him in. And this time, he wouldn't panic when he got her in his arms.

~ * ~

Holly bit her lip when her cell phone lit up and Adam's number appeared on the screen. She let it ring, waiting to pick it up until after she saw the voicemail icon pop up. For a few moments, her heart stuttered with hopeful possibilities.

Unable to wait, she listened to his message, her heart dropping a little more with each word. Certain words and phrases echoed long after she ended the call. *Coffee*, not dinner, not take-out Chinese or sausage, pepperoni, and cheese. *Give me a list*, not "let's get together." There was no mistaking those signals; the back-off message was coming through loud and clear.

Yeah, she had definitely been an idiot for thinking Adam was interested in her as something more than a potential client.

She waited until much later to respond, not wanting to give him another reason to think she wanted more than that. Her pride wouldn't allow it.

Sorry, can't.

Despite the fact that it was three in the morning, Adam replied almost instantly. *Why not?*

Shit. She couldn't pretend she wasn't awake, not when she had just texted him a minute earlier. So much for her brilliant plan.

Tight deadline. It was sort of true. She had promised herself she would finish up the paranormal she was working on by Sunday. There was no need to tell him that she had already submitted a completed draft of her alpha SEAL novel to her editor a full month ahead of schedule.

I understand. Can you take a break for dinner tomorrow? I can pick something up.

Now he mentioned dinner? Obviously, he sensed his fat payday drifting away and was willing to go the extra mile.

No, but thanks, anyway.

~ * ~

Adam stared at the screen, the last of his doubts fading away. She was definitely pissed. He should have called her over the weekend.

Instead of texting, he called her number. She knew that *he* knew she was awake and responding, so unless she was really angry, she would have to answer.

"Yes?"

Adam flinched at the sound of her voice. Instead of her smooth, musical tone, her voice was devoid of feeling. Cold. Very un-Holly-like.

"Holly, I'm sorry about what happened."

"Me, too."

That threw him. What did she have to be sorry for? She wasn't the one who panicked or didn't call even after she said she would.

"For what?"

He heard a soft but weary sigh on the other end. "I'm sorry, Adam. I just don't have the money to put into the cottage right now. I'll definitely keep you in mind, though. Thanks." Holly hung up before he could respond.

Adam stared at the phone for several minutes.

What the hell?

Chapter Seventeen

Adam waited in the hallway for the yoga class to let out. It was a sign of just how desperate he was—willing to risk another run-in with Eve to talk to Holly. Short of showing up on Holly's doorstep, however, which he had considered doing many times over the last several days, he was out of options.

Last night, he had planted himself in Applebee's in the hopes of crossing her path, but her and her friend hadn't shown. After he had witnessed the young female convention amassing in Brandon's section, he understood why.

Now, here he was, skulking in the corridor like some creeper, hoping for a glimpse of Holly while trying to stay below Eve's radar. Luckily, though, Eve appeared to have attached herself to one of the muscled bodybuilders from the weight room and hadn't even looked his way.

"Liz, right?" He stepped out of the shadows as Liz was about to walk past. He glanced down the hallway, but there was no sign of Holly.

Liz paused long enough to wave on a few of the women she had been talking to and faced him. She nodded, eyeing him warily.

"My name is Adam, and—"

"I know who you are. What do you want?"

She wasn't openly hostile, but she wasn't sending out any warm and fuzzies, either. Thankfully, there was no hint of the feminine interest that had flared in her eyes that first night at Applebee's. Thank God for that. The last thing he needed was for any misunderstandings. Unless Holly decided to start taking his calls again, Liz was his best hope for understanding what the hell was going on.

"Can I talk to you for a minute?"

She exhaled and looked longingly at the exit. "Go on."

"Holly's not answering my calls." It was a statement, not a question.

She crossed her arms over her chest and glared at him, waiting. Clearly, she was not going to make this easy for him.

"Do you know why?" he pressed.

She stared at him for a long, few moments. "Holly's my best friend. I don't know you from … yeah, forget I said that. What makes you think I'd betray her confidence?"

Adam blew out a breath. He hadn't thought of that. It just went to show how out of sorts he was. "I don't want you to betray anyone. I just thought … Hell, I don't know what I was thinking." He ran his hand through his hair in a classic gesture of frustration. "I'm sorry."

He turned to go. It had been a mistake to try to approach Holly's friend, both cowardly and stupid. If he had a problem with Holly, and he obviously did, he should be dealing with it himself. He was just going to have to bite the bullet and man-up. He could get her flowers, maybe, and hope it would be enough to earn him a chance to find out how he had managed to fuck up something that had shown more potential than anything else in the last decade.

~ * ~

Liz bit her lip. Holly had been miserable these last few days, and Adam looked no better. Holly was her best friend, and since Liz had been the one to encourage her to go out with Adam in the first place, she felt partially responsible.

Holly had confessed everything the night before. It was the first time in nearly ten years that Holly had wanted to skip their girls' night out, prompting Liz to show up at her door, drag her ass out, and pry the information out of her with a combination of humor and two-for-one drink specials.

Adam certainly wasn't acting like a man who was only interested in Holly as a potential client, and her female spidey senses backed up that assessment. If there was even the slightest chance Holly had made a mistake, a mistake that might be rectified if she would just talk to him, didn't she owe Holly that much?

"Adam, wait." Decision made, she jogged a few steps and caught up to him. If she was wrong, so be it. "I don't know all the details, but Holly thinks you might only be interested in her as a client."

The sheer surprise on his face told her that her instincts had been dead-on. "What? Why would she think that?"

"Apparently, she overheard something."

Adam narrowed his eyes. Liz could practically see the wheels turning.

"It's not true, though, is it?" Liz asked, watching him closely.

"No. Hell no. Look, I did say something like that, but only because I didn't want Eve giving her a hard time."

It was Liz's turn to narrow her eyes. "Eve? Eve Sanderson?"

Adam nodded. "Yeah. You know her?"

Realization dawned in Liz's eyes. A strange expression stole over her face before it blanked completely. "Wait. Let me guess. Eve decided she wants you and won't take no for an answer."

He arched a brow. "Yeah, something like that."

Liz muttered something distinctly unladylike under her breath. "Well, you're not the first she's pulled that crap on, and you probably won't be the last. Unfortunately, if she's set her sights on you, you've got a bull's-eye on your backside until someone else catches her eye."

"A lot of people catch her eye," he grunted.

"Yes, but the only ones she latches on to are the ones who look the other way. As long as she's the one walking away, you're golden. But if *you* do the walking … well, let's just say Eve doesn't handle rejection well."

"How do you know so much about her?"

For a brief moment, the mask cracked and Liz grimaced as though in pain. "Let's just say I have my own personal history with Eve. The question now is: what are we going to do about Holly?"

She glanced down the hall, seeing the bodybuilder showing off to a younger girl while Eve glared at them, looking like steam was about to come out of her ears at any second. If what Adam had said was true, and Liz had no reason to think otherwise, Eve might spot him and forget about the bodybuilder. She had to get him out of there … fast.

"Come on," she said, grabbing his forearm and leading him toward the exit. "We'll talk about it over coffee. You're buying."

Chapter Eighteen

Adam hadn't felt this nervous since the first time he'd had sex. He had been sixteen at the time, though he had looked old enough that, when he told the pretty co-ed he was a junior, she had assumed he was talking about the university. He might have been young and inexperienced, but he hadn't been stupid enough to correct her.

He knocked again with one hand and gripped the roses tightly with the other, inadvertently crushing the stems. A missed thorn dug into his flesh, but the minor pain was a welcome diversion.

"Holly, I know you're in there. Please answer the door."

His coffee with Liz had been enlightening, to say the least, though kind of scary, too. Unlike Holly, Liz had absolutely no problem saying exactly what was on her mind. She had asked Adam point-blank what his intentions were with Holly. When he had blurted out the truth, she had told Adam, in no uncertain terms, exactly what he had to do.

She had then smirked when his face had turned the color of a turnip and his jaw had hit the table, but hadn't wavered for even a moment. Once he had gotten over his initial shock, he had to admire her absolute confidence.

And hope to hell she was right.

~ * ~

"It's late, Adam," Holly said wearily, opening the door a few inches. Obviously sitting in the dark and ignoring his repeated knocks was not conveying the message any more effectively than the unanswered texts and calls. "What do you want?"

Adam used his much larger body and pressed forward. She stepped back, tilting her face upward toward his.

His blue eyes were dark and intense, his movements deliberate. Pure male power radiated off him in waves, making her innermost parts clench against her will. But it was nothing compared to the next words out of his mouth.

"I want *you*, Holly."

She gasped slightly. Disbelief, hope, and a big surge of lust rose up inside her, drowning out her rational mind's increasingly weak protests that Adam was not interested in her that way.

"Apparently, I've done a piss-poor job of

letting you know that my interest in you is anything but professional, and I'm here to set that record straight right now." He tossed the flowers off to the side, red and pink blooms scattering to the floor.

He brought flowers?

She barely had time to process that thought before he was stepping forward again, right into her personal space. She countered by taking another step back, though the length of her stride was less than half his.

"If you have a problem with that, now is the time to say so, Holly. Say the word, and I'll go."

Did she have a problem with that? Her thundering heart and beading nipples didn't think so.

He waited through several of those thundering heartbeats before she whispered, "No. Don't go."

He grinned wolfishly and took another step. So did she.

One more, and he was close enough to reach out, wrap his arm around her waist, and pull her against his hard body. She closed her eyes for just a moment, relishing the feel of all that hardness, the heat seeping through his clothes and hers, and the scent of clean, powerful male. Her nipples grew to diamond-hard tips against his ripped torso, easily distinguishable through the thin material of her ratty tee-shirt.

Without permission, a slight moan managed to escape. He took full and instant advantage, lowering his head to claim her mouth. At the same time, she felt his large hand skim along the curve of her waist and over her hips, pausing only when he cupped her ass and lifted her, drawing her tightly against something incredibly large and extremely rigid.

It felt so right to be fitted against all those hard ridges and bumps. Her much softer, feminine parts yielded instantly to his much harder planes, filling in every dip and curve.

She moved her hand between them, flattening her palm against his chest. Not in an attempt to push him away, but to curl her nails into his chest like tiny claws, fierce and possessive. He rewarded her by thrusting his tongue into her mouth.

She wanted more, so much more, of him thrusting parts of him into parts of her.

Suddenly, her feet were no longer on the ground. She was in Adam's powerful arms, being drawn even closer until every possible inch of her sensitized flesh was pressed against his granite hardness. Total surrender was a given as he ravished her mouth mercilessly, taking as much as he gave, capturing her throaty moans for his own.

Then they were moving. Without easing his grip, Adam walked them forward until her back was against the wall, using his weight to pin her in place. It felt so good, all that pressure, all that unyielding strength against the thousands of nerve endings crying out for his touch.

She felt a rush of cool air as he reached down

between them to grasp the hem of her shirt, felt his rough calluses skimming over her heated skin.

His palm paused briefly over her heart. Surely, he must have felt it thrusting itself against her ribs.

When he smiled against her mouth, she knew he had.

"Say no and I'll stop."

"I'm not saying no, Adam."

He pushed his big, muscular thigh between hers, holding her in place as it pressed suggestively against yet another part of her shamelessly begging for his attention. She tried in vain to flex her hips to relieve some of the ache, but he only pressed harder, letting her know that he was the one in control, and she was all but powerless to stop him.

Why, for the life of her, would she even want to?

Something niggled at the back of her mind, some faint echo of warning, but it was lost in the flood of endorphins as he moved his hand upward, cupping one of her breasts through the thin bra cup.

He growled then, a purely masculine sound that she felt as much as heard. Though she wouldn't have thought it possible, her breasts swelled even more, the hard beads of her nipples pressing forward.

It was both heaven and hell the way he teased her, rubbing his thumbs over them several times before giving a skillful flick of his fingers to release the front clasp of her bra. The soft support vanished, the cups peeled aside and were mercifully replaced with his hot, rough hands. She *might* have whimpered.

"So fucking beautiful," he hissed, releasing her mouth and dropping his head to suckle her through the thin cotton of her tee-shirt. This time, there was no mistaking the sounds she made, crying out at the hard pull of his mouth, not in pain, but in pleasure.

When he nipped her tender skin, she understood instinctively that it was a mark of his approval. A few heartbeats later, he grasped the waistband of her lounge pants and pushed down hard.

"Wrap your legs around me," he commanded, his voice husky and thick with need.

Holly obeyed without question, eagerly stepping out of her pants and snaking her arms around his neck.

She nearly cried out when she felt his fingers between her legs; his groan another sign of his approval at finding her slick and oh-so-wet.

For one interminably long moment, he pulled away from her. She was about to protest until she heard the glorious sound of a snap and a zipper, followed by the tear of foil. Then he was back, grinding his hips against hers, lubricating the proof of his desire with what she had provided. It wasn't *enough*.

She dug her nails into his shoulders, needing *more*.

Thank God he seemed to understand. A slight tilt of his hips poised the blunt head right at her entrance.

He paused, breathing hard. "Holly ..."

Why had he stopped?

She looked into his eyes and saw the raw, stark need matching her own, as well as his unspoken question. She knew instinctively that it was the last time he would ask. Her answer would determine not just the next few minutes, but their future.

"Yes ..." she answered in a husky whisper, using her legs to pull him closer.

Adam pressed forward, penetrating the wet, silken need that had become the focal point of her entire body.

"Oh, fucking hell," he murmured as he worked his way deeper.

This time it was Holly who rewarded him with another rush of silken heat and a tight squeeze made possible by years of Kegel exercises. Judging by the strangled moan that erupted from his throat, they were worth every second.

When his balls pressed against her swollen folds, he paused, a single brief moment only. For that moment, time and space ceased, hung in a suspended sense of nearly unbearable anticipation.

She looked into his eyes, now polished sapphires, and whispered the only word she was capable of. "*Please*."

Adam grunted in affirmation. He withdrew and

thrust again and again with long, thorough strokes that stretched her to her physical limits and filled her completely. It still wasn't enough. He was holding back, and she needed him, all of him.

A minute later, she tightened her leg-lock around his hips and dug her heels into his tight ass in an unspoken request for *more*.

He gave it to her. Increasing his pace, his hips pistons of even greater force, thrusting into her harder and faster. Possessing her. Owning her.

"Yes!" she scream-moaned, grabbing the hair at the base of his skull and tugging hard. This was exactly what she had needed. Him. Pounding into her as if he would die if he didn't. Assuming total control over his pleasure and hers.

"Come for me, Holly," he commanded sharply, grinding his hips, pushing deeper, demanding more. "Come all over my cock, baby."

His raw words undid her. Seconds later, her entire body clenched, a silent scream ripping from her throat.

Adam roared her name as her channel bore down hard around him in complete bliss. He was no longer pumping but pushing hard into and against her as if he couldn't get deep enough.

Along with the intense climax ripping through her body, she felt the pulse of his release as he exploded inside her. Then they were moving again.

Adam's arms were still around her, tight bands that kept her from floating away in thousands of tiny pieces. He dropped down onto the sofa, pulling her with him.

"Jesus, Holly," he moaned, holding her tightly encased in his arms.

She moaned against his neck, her body still shuddering with aftershocks.

"Five minutes ..." she breathed before giving in to the darkness.

Chapter Nineteen

Adam woke up and looked at the clock. Six a.m. If it were any other Friday, he would be up, showered, and eating breakfast by now, checking out the day's schedule and making sure everyone was where they were supposed to be. The guys he worked with were good—Adam only used the best—but it paid to be on top of things.

He wasn't the one on top now. A lush, feminine body was draped over him, legs and arms curled possessively around his body. Her face was buried in his neck, lips parted just enough in exhausted slumber that he could feel the hot, rhythmic puffs of breath against his pulse. She was very warm, his own personal electric blanket. He chuckled, thinking that, come winter, they would be saving a lot on heating bills.

Yes, he was thinking that far ahead, because the last twelve hours had made his future crystal clear.

The slight movement had Holly stirring.

She skimmed her hand down his body and cupped as much of his package as she could. "You're taking the day off," she grumbled against his skin. Her little growl was every bit as possessive as her hand.

His chest swelled with something he had doubted he would ever feel.

He wasn't going anywhere. Not until he had imprinted himself on every inch of her, inside and out, and she knew with absolute certainty that they belonged together. He had made significant progress last night.

After their first time in her living room, they had moved to the bedroom and continued at a more leisurely but no less desperate pace.

Five, he decided, was his new lucky number. A five-minute orgasm. Making her come five times in as many hours.

Yeah. Five was fucking awesome.

"I have a job," he teased.

Holly lifted her head enough to lick along his jawline. "Yes, you do."

In her capable hand, his cock hardened and swelled.

She had an incredible morning voice, husky and low, twisting his insides into a tangle of hot, instant need. Adam closed his eyes and let it wash over him, relishing every second.

And it wasn't because sex with her was better than any he had ever had. It was how he felt *now*, the morning after, that really did it for him. The certain knowledge that he wanted to wake up like this every morning for the rest of his life. That, and the fact that such knowledge filled him with a profound sense of peace instead of scaring the shit out of him, convinced him that it didn't get more right.

As he pondered such things, Holly began to move. She brushed her lips lightly over his, then trailed back down along his jaw. She made soft, little sounds of pleasure as she progressed, as if she was getting as much out of this as he was.

He lazily kneaded her back and her perfect backside encouragingly.

The woman was pure magic. Before long, he was once again lost in the sensations of her intoxicating kisses, the feel of her warm weight moving over him, and all that lush softness beneath his worshipping hands.

It wasn't until he gripped nothing but hair that he realized her intent. All the hazy warm and fuzzies cleared instantly, and a sharp and sudden bolt of lust scored the length of his body.

Fisting her cherry-cola curls, he raised his head to see her wedging between his thighs.

She didn't bother to look back at him. Holly's attention was fully focused on that part of him right in front of her face.

With one finger, she traced the length of him, from base to tip, causing his hips to involuntarily jerk.

From one fucking finger.

That one finger was joined by others until she closed her skillful hand around him and they all began stroking together. She kept her other hand similarly employed, cupping his balls, tugging lightly and rolling, all at the same time. Holy hell, where did she learn *that*?

Then she peeked her tongue out from those soft pink lips and licked at the pre-come beading along the top of his head. She must have liked it because she made an appreciative noise and, seconds later, the first few inches of his cock disappeared into her mouth.

In a flurry of sensations that threatened to blow his mind, the heat of her mouth, the stroke of her tongue, and the light, erotic rasp of her teeth conspired against him.

After several, agonizing seconds, she just … stopped. Why had she stopped?

He opened his eyes and looked down to find her looking back at him, her green eyes filled with lust and something primal and possessive.

"Mine," she growled. "I can taste myself on you, Adam. You're mine."

Fuck yes. His inner caveman tossed aside his club and kneeled before her in absolute submission.

She renewed her efforts with great enthusiasm,

claiming him as he had claimed her. He could have fought it, but why would he? She was right. He *was* hers. And if she felt the need to prove it to him so thoroughly, who was he to deny her?

She owned him. Owned his cock, his heart and, in that moment, his soul.

Hours later, after three meals, two showers, and several more orgasms, Adam woke up again, but alone this time.

The room was dark. A brief look toward the window confirmed that it was well past sunset.

Adam rose, feeling both sated and needy. Physically, he was more than satisfied. Holly had seen to that. But there was another part of him now that would never be fully satisfied. That part needed to see her, to know that she was near and safe, to look into her eyes and feel that incredible rush of connection that made him think crazy, permanent thoughts.

He found her in the kitchen, sitting at the table with her laptop in front of her, the glow from the screen reflected in her eyes. Max was curled up at her feet.

She looked adorable sitting there, with her tousled curls and unmistakable just-fucked looked, fingers flying across the keyboard so quickly they looked blurry from where he stood.

He leaned against the doorframe, content to just watch her. A strange feeling came over him in those moments, like déjà vu, but just the opposite. Instead of feeling like he had experienced this before, he knew he was seeing his future. That there would be hundreds, if not thousands, of nights he would wake up and find her here, just like this.

She paused long enough to take a sip from the mug beside her, and that was when she spotted him. Her features softened, her eyes sparkled, and her lips curved into a smile that made his heart stop altogether.

"Hi," she said softly.

"Hi," he replied. "Writing?"

"Yeah," she confessed. The creeping, rosy blush across her cheeks gave him a pretty good idea of what she was writing about. "I wanted to get a few ideas down while they were still fresh in my mind."

Ideas that he had inspired? Oh yeah, he was all about the inspiration.

He pushed off from the frame. "Yeah? Like what?"

She watched him stalk across the kitchen, her eyes like brands as they scanned down his chest, his hips, his legs, and back up again. He loved it, loved the fierce gleam in her eye, the sense of being wanted like that by her.

"Feelings, mostly. Sensations. Stuff like that."

"Hmmm," he hummed. "You put that into your books, huh?"

"Oh yeah," she said, her voice slightly breathier than it had been only a minute earlier. He loved that he had this kind of effect on her, too. "Being able to capture that separates the good writers from the great ones. Readers can tell the difference."

He stopped beside her, close enough that he could feel the heat radiating from her skin. "Is that so?"

~ * ~

Holly licked her bottom lip. Sitting as she was, her mouth was right in line with his hips. There was no mistaking the large bulge beneath the faded denim. She closed her eyes, remembering what he had looked like naked. The satiny steel feel of him in her hands, between her thighs, in her mouth.

"Yeah. Well, that and lots of research."

"Research." His eyes twinkled with amusement and something else. Something dark and hungry and possessive that had tendrils of heat licking up from her center. Again.

She swallowed. "Yeah."

"Anything in particular you need to research?" he asked, dropping smoothly to his knees and turning her chair to face him. His big hands landed on bare skin just above her knees. She inhaled sharply, her body zinging with anticipation when she realized his intent.

"Um ..." She didn't say it. She couldn't. It was one thing to write about it, to imagine it, to dream of it, but to ask for it? With Adam, Holly had been bolder than she had ever been, but not even she could bring herself to speak of ... *that*.

The part of her that had so brazenly claimed him earlier was nowhere to be found. She was probably taking a well-deserved rest while leaving her sweet, docile alter ego in charge. If vocalizing that particular fantasy was a prerequisite for actually experiencing it, she would be going without.

Thankfully, Adam seemed to understand. He flexed and pressed his hands, guiding her legs open to wedge his big body between them.

"Relax," he whispered, massaging her thighs when they tensed.

Easy for him to say, she thought, barely containing the hysterical giggle trying to erupt. No man had ever done *that* before. She read about it plenty, even wrote about it herself, but that was romantic *fiction*. It was called that for a reason.

She was just about to tell him to stop when he placed a kiss on the inside of her thigh. She had never realized just how sensitive her skin was there. She could feel everything. The silky caress of his hair, the heat of his breath, the stark contrast of his soft lips to the prickly stubble along his jaw.

Without conscious thought, she tangled her fingers into his hair and slid her behind to the front of the chair in silent demand. Her mind might be a little freaked out, but her body was totally on board with where he was going.

Adam thumbed her instep—who knew *that* was an erogenous zone?—and guided her foot to his shoulder. Then he did the same with her other leg. She tilted her head back and watched him through heavy-lidded eyes. How absolutely male he looked there between her legs with his rugged, stubbly features framed by her just-shaved, baby smooth thighs.

Her logical, rational self made one final rally before her inner harlot awoke and took over completely.

"Adam," she breathed. "You don't have to— *ungh* …"

The words broke off with a strangled gurgle when Adam surged forward, licking along her slick folds.

Her head flew back, and all she could think about was how glad she was that she hadn't bothered to put on panties because it would have delayed *this* for several interminable seconds.

"Mmm … You taste so fucking good, baby. Sweet and rich and perfect."

The man was a hummer, and it was amazing. The vibrations skittered across bundles of lovingly abused nerves, more pleasing than Vinny had ever been. And Vinny had never talked to her, either. She would never again underestimate the power of sexy, dirty dialogue while doing sexy, dirty deeds.

The man had some serious skills! He licked, he flicked, he sucked, he fucked her with his tongue.

And just when she thought she couldn't possibly stand another freaking second, he thrust his long, thick fingers deep inside, curling and applying pressure right *there* while he sucked hard on her clit and made her body explode into thousands of tiny scattered pieces of light.

"Damn, that was hot, baby." Holly heard his voice, but she didn't have the strength to open her eyes just yet. It was enough to be held in his arms as he gently rocked her back down to earth. No, not rocking. Walking.

She smiled, or at least thought she did. Humming as she was from that last incredible orgasm, she wasn't quite sure she had complete control over any muscles whatsoever.

"I need to be inside you. Now."

That penetrated the haze. Impossibly, her still tingling sex went from satisfied to needy at the husky rasp of his voice.

After a brief moment of weightlessness, she felt the bed beneath her. Then Adam was above her, hot and hard and naked, sliding deeply inside. They both let out a moan at the same time.

Holly arched and tilted her hips, still reeling from that last orgasm as he pushed farther. Like the very first time, there was no hesitation, no gentle possession. Just raw, blinding need.

He pumped inside her, flesh slapping flesh as he drove himself deeper, only to withdraw and do it again and again. Her climax came fast and hard, shattering her into pieces all over again. Only this time, the pulsing of his sheathed cock deep in her core told her that he had joined her.

She must have zoned out there for a few minutes, because the next thing she knew, Adam was chuckling.

"What's so funny?" she asked dreamily. Maybe if she hadn't been loved repeatedly into a sense of complete and total lassitude, she might have felt a bit offended or at least a little self-conscious. As it was, she just didn't have the strength.

"I was just thinking how lucky I am," he told her. "I don't think helping you with your research would be nearly as much fun if you were still an analyst."

She managed a tired but happy grin. "Bits and bytes don't turn you on?"

"Your bits and bytes do. There are several bits I'd like to bite right now, as a matter of fact," he growled, lowering his head to nip at her breast.

"It really doesn't bother you?" she asked softly, running her hand over his hair in a comforting gesture.

He kissed his way back up to her face. "Having a beautiful, smart, sexy, creative, successful woman as my own? No, Holly, it doesn't bother me. It makes me feel like the luckiest man in the world." In case she needed more convincing, he lowered his mouth to hers, expressing himself with a searing, lingering kiss.

"What about you?" he asked. "Can you be happy with a humble contractor?"

"Oh, yes," she whispered, her words filled with genuine awe and wonderment as she guided him into her again. "You're my Five-Minute Man ..."

~ * ~

Adam groaned, offering a silent prayer of thanks to Liz. "You want to convince Holly she's the one?" she had said to him. "Be her Five-Minute Man. Prove it to her."

He'd had his doubts. After all, Holly wrote romances. Shouldn't he be buying roses and taking her out to candlelight dinners? When he had asked that, Liz had snorted, telling him with unwavering confidence that all that stuff would mean nothing unless Holly believed it was *real*, and there was only one way to do that.

It looked as if Liz had hit the nail on the head with that one.

"Yes, I am," he agreed, flipping them so she was on top of him again. "And you are my Five-Minute Woman."

She purred at that, curling her nails lightly into his chest as she made slow circles with her hips.

"Always. But now, I think I want a lot more than five minutes ..."

Chapter Twenty

"Hello, Adam."

Adam cringed at hearing Eve's sex-kitten purr clearly through his mobile. Having just left Holly's after a long weekend of sheer bliss, he hadn't been thinking clearly or he would have checked the caller ID before answering.

"What do you want, Eve?"

"Is that any way to talk to your lover?"

"We are not lovers," he said through clenched teeth.

"I beg to differ." She laughed softly, undeterred.

She could beg all she wanted. Adam was done. Had been for a long time.

"We had sex, Eve. It was one night. Don't make it out to be anything more than that."

"Keep telling yourself that, baby, but I know better. You and I, we're meant to be. You will accept that eventually."

"I'm hanging up now."

"Okay," she said in a sing-song voice. Her easy agreement set off warning bells in the back of his mind. "But if you do, you might lose your chance to get a bid in on that old gamekeeper's cottage you were so interested in."

Adam's thumb paused over the "End Call" button. "What the hell are you talking about, Eve? The cottage was sold months ago." *To Holly.*

"What if I told you the Historical Society is trying to buy back the property?"

"Won't happen," he said without thinking. "I know the owner, and she's not interested in selling."

There was a long pause, long enough for him to realize his mistake.

"She, huh? So that's who has captured your attention," Eve mused. "I should have known. Is she the one you have been *doing business with* lately, Adam?"

Fuck! He needed to get his head out of his pants and start thinking with his brain again. If Eve thought for a minute that Adam was interested in anyone besides her, she would make Holly's life a living hell. Things were too new, too fresh with Holly to subject her to that kind of insanity yet. He had to make Eve believe that Holly was not a threat, at least until he could figure out a more permanent solution.

"We've met," he admitted, carefully choosing

his next words. "She was interested in a professional opinion."

"Is that all?" Eve asked doubtfully. In his mind's eye, he could picture her eyes narrowing and her brows drawing together as she tried to gauge his sincerity. At that moment, he was intensely glad they were not face to face because, after three incredible days with Holly, there was no way he would be able to school his features enough to make anyone believe Holly was anything less than what she was—*the one*. Eve didn't need to know that yet.

There were very few women who worried Adam. Eve was one of them. Her behavior over the past six months clearly proved she had a borderline obsessive, and delusional, personality.

"Did she hire you, Adam?" Eve's voice brought him back to the moment.

"No." That, at least, he could answer honestly. He would be working on the cottage all right, but not as hired help. But … this might be a way to get Eve out of attack mode. If he could manage to give Eve the impression that he had just done a consult and wouldn't be involved any further, it might buy him enough time to work out a better, permanent solution. "She said she would keep me in mind, though."

"I was hoping you would say that."

Rather than the rush of relief he had been hoping for, a stone the size of Mount Rushmore settled in his stomach. "Why is that?"

"Because the place was part of the original William Penn estate, so the Historical Society has a vested interest in ensuring that any and all renovations are performed under strict, historically accurate guidelines. If *you* were doing the renovations, we would know they were being done properly and have no basis for forcing the sale."

Double fuck! Adam closed his eyes, willing himself to remain calm. How did he keep managing to fuck this up? When would he learn not to underestimate Eve? His mind worked frantically. He did not want her anywhere near Holly.

"It is only the Society's business if the owner petitioned to have the site recognized as a historical landmark. Has such a petition been made?"

God, he hoped not. He was fairly certain Holly had not done so. In the first place, Holly would have mentioned it when she had given him the grand tour and talked about the research she had been doing. And in that second, he really couldn't see her wanting that kind of attention. Historically registered landmarks, even those privately owned, had a tendency to draw interest from history buffs, researchers, and tourists. Holly, like him, liked her privacy.

"Oh, Adam." Eve laughed softly, her voice carrying a barely concealed warning. "Not everything is done by the book, you know. Sometimes, you have to go above and beyond to get what you really want."

A shiver went down his spine. He knew they were no longer just talking about the cottage. Despite his good intentions, Eve hadn't been convinced.

"Eve, you leave—"

She was still laughing when she disconnected the call.

~ * ~

"Adam, is there something you want to tell me?" Holly asked, concern in her eyes as she stroked her hand over his chest.

They lay side by side, still coming down from their incredible love-making. Ever since he had come to pick her up for her "surprise date," a sunset cruise aboard his personal fishing/cruising boat on the nearby lake, he had seemed distracted.

"No," he said far too quickly to be believable. "Why?"

She pressed a kiss to his skin. The lake had been perfect, as had the picnic dinner he had brought along. The moment they had returned to her place, he had wasted no time in relieving her of her clothes and making tender, passionate love to her. As wonderful as it had been, something felt off.

"Just a feeling, I guess." She sighed. "I'm sorry. I'm not really very good at this."

He tightened his arm around her as he pressed a kiss to the top of her head. "You are perfect," he said. "And perceptive. I just have a lot on my mind lately."

"Anything I can help with?" she asked, pushing him from his side onto his stomach. He allowed it. She straddled his hips, resting her sex against his perfect man ass as she leaned forward to knead the tight knots around his upper back and shoulders. Damn, but the man had the sexiest back she had ever seen. Wide at the top, defined from years of construction work, then tapering down into lean hips.

"Yeah. Keep doing that," he groaned into the pillow. "Damn, that feels good."

She remained quiet for several long minutes, using her hands to leisurely map and memorize this part of him she didn't get to see nearly often enough. "If you were having second thoughts, you'd tell me, wouldn't you?"

He shifted beneath her, rolling to his back. "I'm not having second thoughts, Holly."

"But if you *were*, you'd tell me, right?"

She hated feeling this needy. As far as relationships went, she was pitiful. A man like Adam would not appreciate a clingy, needy woman, but she just couldn't help herself. He—this— seemed too good to be true, and she needed validation.

Adam rested his hands just above her hips, holding her in place. He flexed his hands, squeezing lightly until her eyes met his. "Yes. But I'm not."

He lifted her as if she weighed nothing, and she sighed in both relief and pleasure as he guided her back down onto him, filling more than her body.

Words were one thing, but he was what she really needed. There was no mistaking the reassurance this connection brought with it. With Adam, it wasn't just sex. If it ever began to feel like it was, that was when she would really start to worry.

For now, she was content to push the sense of disquiet far to the back of her mind and trust her heart. And Adam.

Chapter Twenty-One

Holly heard a knock at the door. Glancing away from her screen, she looked up at the burnished brass clock on the wall and frowned. It was early afternoon. The only two people for whom she would be willing to interrupt her writing groove— Liz and Adam—would be at work for another couple hours. The postman had already dropped off the mail for the day, and she wasn't expecting any packages.

"Ignore it," she said to Max, who swiveled his gaze between her and the front of the house. Unlike other dogs, he didn't bark at the door if Holly was around. He always looked to her first.

After a few seconds of silence, she turned her attention back to her computer and reread the last couple sentences to continue where she had left off, right in the middle of a really intense scene where her lead female character had seen her love interest shift into a beast for the first time. She had been on such a roll that she hadn't even taken a break to pee for the last three hours.

Her fingers had barely touched the keys when the irritating knock came again.

"Go away," Holly mumbled under her breath. What was it with people? If they knocked and no one answered, it meant that either, a) no one was home, or b) no one wanted to open the damn door.

Five minutes passed. Still, the incessant knocking continued. Whoever it was, they were persistent. And had just taken the express route right to the very top of Holly's shit list.

Her concentration shattered, Holly got up and went to the door, ready to give whoever it was a much-needed lesson in socially acceptable behavior.

When Holly opened the door, however, the words evaporated on her lips. Standing on her front porch was Swedish Barbie, dressed in an expensive-looking, ass-hugging skirt and matching jacket. Her blonde hair was pulled back in a perfectly smooth bun with nary a hair out of place. Her makeup was so well done her Nordic features appeared airbrushed.

"Holly McTierney?" Barbie asked doubtfully, her gaze raking down and back up in blatant perusal.

Devoid of makeup, wearing one of Adam's T-shirts and her super comfy pajama pants, Holly knew she didn't look presentable enough to receive visitors, especially not ones who looked like they had just stepped out of the pages of a fashion magazine. Which, of course, was one of the many reasons she hadn't wanted to open the door in the first place.

"Yes."

Holly kept her hand on the door, allowing it to open only wide enough for her and Max to check out who had so rudely interrupted their afternoon. That didn't stop Swedish Barbie from nosily looking over Holly's shoulder and into the house, an easy thing to do since she was a good nine or ten inches taller than Holly.

"May I come in?"

Holly leaned against the door. "I'm a little busy right now. What do you want?"

Barbie managed what was no doubt intended to be a friendly smile, but her eyes were anything but. Holly wondered if the woman knew about her and Adam. She had meant to ask Adam about her, given the exchange she had inadvertently witnessed at the Y, but it hadn't come up. They had been too busy doing other, much more pleasurable things. And the few times she had thought about it, she hadn't wanted to ruin the mood.

"My name is Eve Sanderson. I'm with the Covendale Valley Historical Society."

Holly blinked but said nothing. She was vaguely familiar with the Society. Shortly after she had purchased the place, they had started sending her letters, asking for permission to inspect the property and include it as part of their colonial history tours. The thought of strangers poking around her house and busloads of school children traipsing over her lawn had her dismissing the idea pretty quickly.

"Despite our repeated attempts to contact you, you have not responded," Eve continued. "You did receive several letters from us, did you not?"

"I did, and I did respond. I'm not interested." She had only responded to the first letter. Each subsequent one went right into the paper shredder the moment she had ensured all staples had been safely removed.

Eve forced another small smile. "Then you are aware of the rich history of this particular parcel, and the Society's desire to have it registered as a historical landmark."

"I am. And the answer is still no." Holly took a step back and began to close the door, when Eve put her hand out to stop it.

"Perhaps you do not understand the significance," Eve began, her voice dripping with barely concealed condescension.

"No, I think it is *you* who does not understand," Holly said firmly. Her searing gaze went to Eve's hand. "I will say this one more time for you very slowly so you can keep up. *I. Am Not. Interested.*"

Expression thunderous, Eve narrowed her eyes. For a few moments, Holly thought Eve-Barbie might actually attack her. Holly kind of hoped she would. While not normally a violent person, there was something immensely appealing about taking Miss High-and-Mighty down a peg or two. It wouldn't even have to be anything big, really, just enough to let Eve-Barbie know she wasn't about to be pushed around by some Swedish supermodel wannabe.

Instead, her unwelcome visitor smoothed her features back into a semi-professional mask and smiled coldly. "You're new here, so let me give you a piece of helpful advice. The Covendale Valley Historical Society has the backing of some very powerful members of this community who want to ensure that our local history is preserved for future generations. If I were you, I would think twice about engaging in a battle you can't win." Eve's eyes practically glowed. "We care for and protect what is ours."

A chill ran up and down the length of Holly's spine as every one of her female senses flared to life. With a scary certainty, she knew they were no longer simply talking about the cottage.

Visions of Eve's hand running along Adam's bicep with serious familiarity clouded her vision for a moment, before she pushed them back. Anything he'd had with Eve must be over, right? Because Adam had been spending his evenings and weekends with her, not Eve.

Eve was probably just reluctant to let him go.

Holly could understand that. She wouldn't let Adam go easily, either.

"Let me make this perfectly clear so there is no doubt. *I* am the legal owner of this house and the land surrounding it. I have no intention of applying for any historical recognition whatsoever, nor will I. This is private property. And *I* care for and protect what is *mine*."

~ * ~

Later that night, Holly was still bristling over Eve Sanderson's unexpected visit.

"Are you having a drink tonight?" Holly asked Liz as the server appeared to take their drink orders. "Because I am definitely having a drink tonight."

"Unsweetened red wine for me," Liz told the young man without opening the beverage menu. "Whatever you have is fine."

The server turned to Holly. "And you, ma'am?"

Holly pointed to the brightly colored photo image splashed across the cover of the laminated stand-up card. "Jack Daniels Tennessee Honey."

The waiter didn't bother looking up from his little pad. He was young like Brandon, but not nearly as friendly. He looked extremely bored. "Want that with the blackberry lemonade and ginger ale?"

"Whatever. Just make sure it's a double shot."

He nodded and left, leaving Liz staring

worriedly from across the table. "A double? What's up?"

Holly grimaced. "Remember I told you about that woman I saw with Adam at the Y that night? Well, she showed up on my doorstep today."

"Eve came to your house?"

Holly stared at her friend in disbelief. She had never told Liz the woman's name. She hadn't known it herself until a few hours ago. "*Eve*? You mean you *know* her?"

Liz grimaced. "Yeah, I know her, all right. She is bad news, Holly."

"Why didn't you say anything before? Like when I told you what happened? That could have been useful information, Liz."

"Because I didn't know then that the woman you saw was Eve. I didn't find out until after Adam told me."

Holly shook her head. This vague fog of confusion was supposed to come after the double shot, not before. "Wait. You talked to Adam? When?"

Guilt suffused Liz's features. "Last Wednesday. He kind of cornered me at the Y to find out why you weren't talking to him."

"And you told him?" Holly hissed.

"Well, duh. You were miserable, Holly. I told him why you were upset, the light bulb blinked on, and he explained what really happened. *She* was going after *him*, Holly, not the other way around."

"And you just believed him?" As skeptical as Holly was, Liz was even more so when it came to the kind of bullshit men spewed to save their own asses. More than one dinner conversation had centered around Liz's personal dating experiences. Some of those tales even occasionally found their way into Holly's storylines, because the truth was so often stranger than fiction.

"I'll admit, I was doubtful at first. As soon as I realized that Eve was the other woman, though, I knew he was telling the truth. You should have seen him, Holly. He was every bit as miserable as you were. I had to do something."

The discussion was suspended when the server reappeared with their drinks and a basket of warm, crusty bread. Holly wasted no time in bringing the straw to her lips, relishing the rush of sweet, smooth alcohol over her tongue.

Liz placed her meal order first, then Holly doubled it.

In a shocking move, Liz tore off a piece of bread and slathered it with whipped butter.

"Liz …" Holly said slowly, watching in morbid fascination as Liz savored the forbidden carbs. That, more than anything, told her that Liz was withholding crucial information. "What exactly did you do?"

"Nothing, really," Liz said, avoiding Holly's eyes.

The very distinct red tint infusing her cheeks

suggested otherwise.

"*Liz* ..." Holly warned.

"Oh, all right. I made him buy me a coffee, and I told him that, if he really wanted to rock your world, he needed to be your Five-Minute Man. He, of course, had no idea what that meant, so I had to explain it to him. There. Are you happy now?"

Holly gaped at Liz from across the table. At her best and only friend. She didn't say anything, though. She just pulled her drink closer and continued to draw from the straw, glad she had asked for a double.

Liz kept shooting furtive glances at her, alternately mangling the remaining bread by pulling off bite-sized pieces and sipping her wine.

By the time their meal arrived, they still hadn't spoken. It was Liz who finally broke the silence.

"Are you angry with me?"

Holly exhaled heavily, pushing the now-empty glass off to the side. Her head was buzzing pleasantly, and she was feeling more relaxed. "No, I'm not angry with you. Because of you, I had a three-night, three-day marathon of incredibly hot and wild monkey sex."

Liz's eyes widened. Then, when Holly grinned, they both burst into gales of laughter, drawing stares from the surrounding tables.

"So, I did a good thing?"

"You did a very good thing," Holly agreed. "Adam is ... well, he is the personification of my perfect man." She shook her head. "In fact, he is too good to be true. I knew there had to be a catch. And she showed up on my front porch today."

"Eve is something else, but you can't hold that against Adam. It's not his fault she's a psycho hose beast and can't take no for an answer."

"Psycho   hose   beast?"   Holly   repeated incredulously.

Liz waved her hand dismissively. "I heard it in this really bad 80's film. Never thought I'd actually use it, but in this case, it fits."

"Tell me."

Liz scowled. "Let's just say I have a good reason to hate Eve Sanderson and leave it at that."

Holly wanted to ask more, but the look of resolve on Liz's face told her she wouldn't get much more out of her on the subject. Thankfully, their meals arrived and gave them something else to focus on.

Chapter Twenty-Two

Adam cursed when the stubborn oil valve gave way, covering his forearm in the dark, thick liquid. Changing the oil on his truck was child's play, something he had done dozens of times, but it was hard to concentrate when he was so distracted.

It was Tuesday night, and Holly was out with her friend. Would Liz tell Holly about running into him at the Y? About their shocking and revelatory discussion at the coffee shop?

Yeah, she probably would. Liz had made it no secret that Holly was more like a sister to her than a friend, and sisters definitely shared that kind of shit. At least *his* sisters did. Growing up, he had overheard a lot more girl talk than he had wanted to. Frank and explicit discussions on everything from makeup to boys and everything in-between.

How would Holly react? Would she be upset with Liz for revealing extremely personal and useful information, or would she understand that Liz had only her best interests at heart? Knowing Holly, it was probably the latter. Holly might be somewhat of a loner, but she was fiercely loyal to those few she had chosen to allow into her inner circle. A circle that now hopefully included him.

Either way, it was probably better for everyone involved if they *did* talk about it and got it out in the open. He would have done so himself but, like most guys, he wasn't good at that kind of sharing shit. He preferred to speak more through actions than words.

Undoubtedly, Liz would have a better idea of how to say things to make Holly understand the truth of it. Besides, with his luck, someone might have seen him and Liz together that night and that might somehow make it back to Holly. He didn't want any more misunderstandings to come between them.

Which brought up the other primary source of his distraction: Eve. He couldn't get that last phone call out of his head. It had been on his mind all day, wondering exactly what she was up to. He thought he had done a fairly good job of shifting Eve's focus away from Holly, but one never knew with Eve. She might give the impression of not being very smart, but the woman could be quite cunning when she put her mind to it. The fact that Eve was using the Historical Society to further her own agenda was proof of that.

Even if she didn't believe Holly was a rival for

his attention, Eve knew that Adam had been interested in obtaining the gamekeeper's cottage at one point. He had mentioned it during their one and only dinner together. Of course, he'd had no idea of what she was capable of then. She had been asking him about his job, and he had casually mentioned that he had a special affinity for doing historical renovations.

It had seemed so unimportant, just a polite, getting-to-know-each-other conversation.

Eve had been thrilled to discover they shared a common interest. She had told him that she had always been fascinated by local history, and that her wealthy, powerful father was on the board of the Covendale Valley Historical Society. They had talked about several local homesteads, and as part of that, he had told her about the cottage, about its history, and his dashed hopes of acquiring it.

How the hell would he have known that bit of seemingly innocuous information would come back to bite him in the ass?

Eve obviously thought the cottage was a way to worm her way back into his life. What she didn't seem to understand was that nothing she said or did would make that happen. One night had been more than enough, and he was still paying for it.

The question was: what should he do about it? Should he attempt to talk to Eve? That particular route had never been successful in the past; Eve only heard what she wanted to hear. Nevertheless, he felt as if he should be doing *something*. Left unchecked, the situation had potential disaster written all over it.

His thoughts went back to Holly, which seemed to happen every few minutes or so. Damn, but he had it bad. She was everything he had ever dreamed of in a woman. Smart, sassy, funny, talented, and she brought him close to seeing God every time they had sex. She was capable and fiercely independent, except when it came to him. She willingly let him take the lead, and he wouldn't have it any other way. *Christ*. The way she melted against him, looked up at him with those big green eyes filled with so much hope and trust and, dare he think it, love.

It seemed too soon to contemplate such a possibility, but there it was. Whether it really was or not remained to be seen, but the potential was there, stronger than it had been in any other relationship he had ever been in.

It was exactly for that reason that he wanted to keep Eve as far away from her as possible. Holly should not have to suffer because he had made some bad choices long before they had ever even met. And, if he was being really honest with himself, he wanted to *be* the man she thought he was when she looked at him like that. The one who would do anything to protect her and keep her safe from the likes of psychologically unbalanced women like Eve Sanderson.

~ * ~

By Thursday, Adam was more than ready to spend the rest of the night with Holly. His arms, and various other parts of his anatomy, ached, and not because he had spent the last two days redoing the stonework around a floor-to-ceiling fireplace dating back nearly two hundred years. No, this pain was born solely of the agonizing want and need to drown in the magical touch of one smart-mouthed little brunette.

He gripped the phone in his hand, the words more disappointing than he could have imagined.

"I'm sorry, Adam," Holly said, sounding as weary as he had ever heard her. "I'm going to have to cancel our dinner tonight." She explained how she had come out of the grocery store to find not one, but two flat tires. "I got a tow, but they don't have the right size tires in stock. They are checking some of their other locations right now. I'm going to be stuck here for a while yet."

It had been three days since he had last seen her. He would be damned if he let it get to four.

"Where are you?"

"Covendale Tire and Auto."

"I'll be there in thirty minutes."

"Adam, you don't have to …" she started to say, but he disconnected before she could finish. He absolutely *did* have to. Holly needed him.

Forgoing a shave, Adam jumped in the shower to rinse off the day's dirt and sweat before pulling on some clean jeans and a shirt. He made it to the garage in record time.

Holly was in the waiting room, worrying her bottom lip and staring blankly at the television mounted on the wall. His heart sped up at the very sight of her. Even in old jeans and a worn college hoodie, she was quite possibly the most beautiful woman he had ever seen.

She turned then, and the look on her face when she spotted him took his breath away. No woman had ever looked at him like that. Like he was the sun after a week's worth of rain. It was an effort not to sprint across the room and crush her to him.

"Adam, you didn't have to come all the way down here." At least, that's what her mouth said. Her eyes told a completely different story.

"I wanted to," he said sincerely, surprised at how normal his voice sounded. "I promised you a dinner, remember?"

"Actually, I promised to cook dinner for *you*," she corrected with an embarrassed smile. "Except, here I am, and your dinner is being held in a refrigerated storage room at the grocery store."

He shrugged. She could hand him a bag of chips from the vending machine and he would be happy. "So? We'll eat out tonight."

She pouted. "I really wanted to cook for you."

Damn, she was so adorable. He was going to

eat *her*. That was what he was really hungry for. He eyed the vinyl and chrome chairs, imagining Holly on one of them, head back, him kneeling on the floor between her spread legs …

"You will, I promise. But, since you've had a pretty rough day, I'm treating you."

She gave him a smile that made his chest and his balls ache at the same time. "My hero," she murmured.

Fuck. She really had to stop looking at him like that or that waiting room fantasy was going to happen. Since there were other people around, one of them a seventy-something grandma eyeing them both with blatant interest, that probably wasn't the best idea.

"Let me talk to the mechanic, then you can tell me all about it over dinner."

~ * ~

"I think this is quite possibly the best burger I've ever had," Holly said later, between mouthfuls. "I can't believe I've never eaten here before."

"Yeah, no place better for burgers than Lou's," he agreed.

The mechanic's words were still buzzing around in his head. Both tires had nails in them. Holly could have picked them up anywhere over the last several days. There had been no blatant sign of tampering, but Adam's gut wasn't convinced.

He kept his voice casual when he asked, "So, tell me; how has the rest of your week been going?"

~ * ~

Holly finished chewing and swallowed, then stalled a bit longer by taking a sip of the heavenly old-fashioned vanilla Coke. It was on the tip of her tongue to tell him about the visit from Swedish Barbie, but she didn't. Liz had been right when she said it wasn't Adam's fault that Eve had a *Fatal Attraction* thing going on.

What Holly hadn't agreed with was Liz's suggestion to tell Adam about Eve's visit. Telling Adam at this point could be counterproductive. First, she really didn't want to come off as the whiny, needy type who needed her man—*her man!*—to fight her battles for her. As unpleasant as Eve was, Holly had no doubt she could handle her.

Second, there was a slim chance that Eve was there for exactly the reason she had said—the Historical Society had a bug up its collective ass about Holly's refusal to involve them in anything to do with the cottage. If that was the case, then involving Adam was pointless. There was nothing he could do about it, and getting him anywhere near Eve unnecessarily was the last thing Holly wanted to do.

"Not too bad." She picked up a french fry, dragging it through the blob of ketchup. "I had a bit of a scare with Max yesterday. He must have gotten into something he shouldn't have and was throwing up all day."

Adam froze with the soft drink in his hand. "How's Max now? Do you need to get home?"

Holly's heart just about melted when that was the first thing Adam said.

"He's doing much better, thanks for asking. Whatever it was, he seems to have gotten it out of his system. I woke up every hour on the hour to check on him, which is why I probably look like roadkill today."

"You look beautiful, Holly."

She blushed, feeling the warmth blossom from somewhere behind her ribcage. No man had ever called her beautiful and sounded like he meant it. Even if he was lying through his teeth, it sounded sincere.

"I'm sorry you had to drive all the way down here."

"No problem. You can always call me. Any time, for any reason. I'm there if you need me. Promise me, Holly. I ... worry about you."

She could tell that the admission wasn't easy for him. As much as she appreciated it, she was not about to become one of *those* women by bothering him over every little thing. She was a big girl.

"You have enough on your mind, Adam. You don't need to worry about me, too."

"Maybe I want to."

Holly looked into his eyes and saw the sincerity there. "You know, Adam, I think that is the nicest thing anyone has ever said to me. Thank you."

If she didn't know better, she could have sworn her rugged alpha male blushed, causing her heart to stutter-step over a few beats.

She reached out and put her hand over his. "But, just so you know, I'm not the Penelope Pitstop damsel-in-distress type."

The corners of his lips quirked. "I know. But a guy likes to feel needed."

Holly's gentle smile grew into a wicked grin. "Well, it just so happens there is something I could use your help with."

"Yeah? What's that?"

Holly crooked her finger to draw him closer. "First," she whispered, "you can give me a ride home. Then"—she paused, running her tongue along her bottom lip sensuously—"you can *give me a ride.*"

Oh, hell yes! Holly thought as Adam immediately signaled for the waitress, scraped the remains of the burgers and fries into a take-home box for Max, and practically dragged Holly out of the diner. They made it as far as his truck before he pushed her up against it and claimed her mouth in a womb-clenching kiss.

"Do you have any idea what your dirty little mouth does to me?" he ground out as he pressed the hard proof of his arousal into her soft belly.

"Dirty little mouth?" She chuckled seductively. "Baby, I write erotic romance for a living. I can do a hell of a lot better than that." She pulled Adam down then whispered dialogue from a scene she had been writing only that morning.

Because she was a firm believer that talk alone was cheap, she then slid her hand down between them and discreetly cupped him as she whispered, feeling him grow even longer and thicker beneath her palm.

Adam shuddered and made a kind of strangled sound in his throat. Then he unceremoniously unlocked the truck and all but tossed her up into the seat.

"Woman, you have no idea what you have just done."

Neither one of them noticed the dark BMW sedan parked in the shadows.

Chapter Twenty-Three

It was amazing what a night of healthy, highly-physical sex could do to relieve tension and stress. For the next twelve hours, Adam had Holly exactly where he wanted her—over, under, and around him—and he didn't spare a thought for sick dogs or flat tires or anything else, for that matter. As long as Holly was in his arms, he knew she was safe.

Getting up for work the next morning wasn't easy. Adam had to drag his tired ass out of a soft, warm bed and an even softer, warmer woman. With a long, lingering kiss and a travel mug of extra-strong coffee, Holly good-naturedly kicked him out. He wasn't sure he would have made it to the job site otherwise.

That was when the worry came back with a vengeance.

Adam had no proof that Eve was behind any of the unfortunate events Holly had faced. Shit happened. Dogs did sometimes get into something they shouldn't. People did pick up nails along the road and get flat tires. If he hadn't had that phone call from Eve, he probably wouldn't have given it any further thought.

But Eve *had* called him, and he couldn't *stop* thinking about it.

Maybe he should have said something to Holly. At least that way she could be on her guard in case Eve really was up to something. As much as he didn't want to worry her unnecessarily, he had her safety to consider.

By mid-afternoon, he had made up his mind. He couldn't get into the whole thing over the phone, but he could tell Holly enough to be aware until he could get there after work and explain everything.

Adam pulled his phone out of his pocket and tapped in Holly's number, frowning when it went to voicemail. She had said she was going to be home all day. Why wasn't she answering?

He tried to keep the irrational panic rising within him at bay. There were a lot of perfectly good reasons for Holly not answering her phone. She could still be sleeping; he had kept her awake most of the night. She could be in the shower. Or exercising with the music blasting. Or outside with Max. Hell, maybe she was writing in the kitchen and had simply turned the volume down on her phone so she could get some good time in without interruptions.

"Holly, this is Adam. Listen, there's something I need to talk to you about. I'll explain everything tonight, but until then, just … be careful, okay? Stay close to home and call me right away if anything weird happens." He was just about to disconnect when he added, "And Holly? Call me back as soon as you get this. Bye."

The afternoon wore on. Every hour lasted longer than the last.

And Holly still hadn't called.

~ * ~

It was official. Holly was falling in love.

That might not have been a completely accurate statement. She was pretty sure she was *already* there, but her rational mind balked at the possibility of such a thing happening so quickly. She might write about love at first sight and soul mates, and assorted romantic fodder, but she wasn't ready to drink her own Kool-Aid just yet.

What she felt for Adam defied logic; that was a given. But whether or not it was the real thing, something that would not only last but continue to grow over the years, remained to be seen. Intense like? Absolutely. Heavy lust? Yep, she was all over that. But *the one*? That was some scary stuff. If she was wrong, it had the potential to be devastating.

As of that moment, however, Holly was riding cloud nine.

After Adam left, she indulged in a long, leisurely shower, one that didn't consist of a thirty-second wash followed by ten minutes of hot shower sex. Every swipe of the bath sponge over her sensitive flesh reminded her of Adam's rigorous attention. She chuckled at that. It turned out Adam really did have a thing for dirty talk. Who knew the skills developed in writing romance novels would have such a profound, practical application in real life?

Craving something more substantial than her usual fruit and granola, Holly took the time to chop up some fresh veggies and made an omelet, which she and Max shared with some whole grain toast.

While they ate, Holly reflected on the last few weeks. Outwardly, not much had changed. She lived in the same house, had the same career, and followed essentially the same daily routine as she had last month. But inside, the changes had been epic.

Holly was happy. Wonderfully, ridiculously happy. The sun shone brighter, the air smelled cleaner, food tasted better, and all because Adam was a part of her life now. It was no longer a matter of waking up, going through the motions, and being satisfied with being content. For the first time, Holly felt like she was truly living, finding joy in even the smallest things. Things that she had previously overlooked or taken for granted.

Like the beautiful morning. Why sit inside

when modern technology afforded the portability to go anywhere?

Feeling deliciously sore in all the right places, her mind still buzzing with Adam-induced endorphins, she made her decision.

Coffee in one hand, laptop in the other, she went out onto her back porch and poured herself into the padded lounge chair. The air was fresh and cool. The skies were clear and blue, almost the exact shade of Adam's eyes. Sunlight filtered through the surrounding trees, creating lace-like patterns of shady greens over the lawn and gardens.

Max curled up beside her on the warm stone patio, his eyes lazily watching the birds and butterflies as they flitted around the blooming day lilies and morning glories. She closed her eyes and tried to capture exactly how she felt at that moment. If she could find the right words to describe what she was feeling, if she could manage to convey that in one of her stories, it would be literary gold.

She must have dozed off at some point, because the next thing she knew, Max was anxiously nuzzling her arm.

"What's up, Max?" she asked drowsily, tangling her fingers in his thick, silky fur. It took a moment before her nose and ears registered the scent of something burning and the distant beep of a smoke alarm.

"What the hell?" Holly bolted upright, automatically saving her latest document and setting her laptop off to the side. She slid the screen door aside and entered the house. The scent was stronger inside, but not overpowering. Holly went from room to room, looking for the source. That was when she realized the smoke was not coming from within, but was wafting through the open windows on the far side of the house.

She looked outside and spotted the smoke pouring out of the small outbuilding where she kept her lawn and garden equipment, and her outdoor tools.

Holly ran back into the kitchen and grabbed the small fire extinguisher she kept there. With Max at her heels, she then hurried across the front of the house.

She had barely placed her hand on the shed's doorknob when there was a loud *boom* from within. An instant later, the windows and doors exploded outward, lifting Holly off her feet and throwing her backward.

A tremendous rush of intense pain burst along the back of her body, and then she wasn't moving anymore.

~ * ~

When Adam's phone buzzed, he breathed a sigh of relief. *Finally!*

"Hey, beautiful." He grinned into the phone. "What took you so long?"

"Now that's more like it."

The voice on the other end wiped the smile away instantly. It wasn't Holly, but Eve. Again. If his business wasn't tied to his mobile, he would have had the number changed months ago. He had even had Brandon show him how to block her number, but Eve must have caught on and called from another.

"What do you want, Eve?" he asked, all traces of warmth having fled with his smile.

"I want to talk to you."

"So talk."

She laughed softly. "Not over the phone, Adam. In person."

"Not interested."

"Oooh," she purred, "you know I love it when you get all growly, Adam. It makes me wet."

Her words disgusted him. How had he ever found her attractive? Now, if Holly had called and said that to him …

"I know about your little author friend, Adam," Eve said, confirming his worst fears and freezing him on the spot. "Honestly, I don't know what you see in her. You are way out of her league."

"Stay away from her, Eve," Adam warned.

"Or what? It's a free country, Adam."

"I'm not kidding, Eve."

"Neither am I," she said, her voice noticeably less sex-kittenish. "Meet me, Adam. One drink, that's all I ask."

"No."

"One drink," she persisted. "And if, after you hear what I have to say, you still feel the same way, I will bow out gracefully."

Adam exhaled. There was absolutely nothing Eve could possibly say that would make him want to get involved with her again. Now that he had found Holly, there was no going back. Holly was everything he wanted in a woman and then some.

"I am not going to change my mind, Eve."

"Then you have nothing to lose, do you? Come on, Adam. One drink. That's not so much to ask, is it?"

Every gut instinct he had told him that this was a really bad idea. It sounded far too easy, and nothing involving Eve was ever that simple. Either she was lying outright, or she had some hidden agenda. Either was a likely possibility.

Yet, there was a part of him that wanted to believe that, deep down, Eve did possess some shred of decency. That after months of unsuccessful attempts to get him back into her life and her bed, she was finally coming to accept the fact that it just wasn't going to happen.

"I have one drink with you, and you promise to finally let this go?" he repeated doubtfully.

"Cross my broken heart."

There was a slight chance she was being sincere; that after one last, final attempt, she would be willing to walk away peacefully. That possibility, however remote, was more appealing than his latest plan of filing a restraining order against her and having Holly do the same. If he could finally put this to rest with one drink and a few minutes of his time, wouldn't it be worth it? And if, as he feared, it didn't work, well, he would talk to Holly that night and get on those restraining orders first thing in the morning.

"All right. One drink. Public place. Where do you want to meet?"

"How about the Lakeside Pub?"

The Lakeside Pub was only about a five-minute drive from where he was. If he left right from the job site, he could meet Eve for one quick drink and still be at Holly's within an hour.

"How long will it take you to get there?"

"I'm already here."

Chapter Twenty-Four

Still wondering if he was doing the right thing, Adam put in a call to Holly. When her voicemail picked up again, he left a quick message, hoping to hell he was not making another huge mistake.

With his clothes coated in plaster powder and sawdust, and his hair stuck to the back of his sweaty neck, Adam managed only a cursory brush-off before walking into the dimly lit bar. He didn't feel self-conscious; Lakeside had been a community staple for over a hundred years and catered to the blue collar working crowd. Those looking for a classier experience used the formal dining entrance on the other side of the building.

He was well-known there, sometimes stopping by with a couple of his guys after work when they were in the area. The bartender, Paul, and a few regulars offered him friendly nods as he made his way over to one of the small tables along the wall.

Given that it was still early, barely past five, the place was fairly empty.

Eve was indeed waiting for him, dressed in a provocative, low-cut sundress that showcased her pin-up girl curves. It was wasted on him. At one time, he might have found her attractive, but sometimes not even the prettiest packaging was enough to hide the ugliness inside. He found the pitcher of beer, two large frosty mugs, and filled shot glasses sitting on the table far more interesting.

Eve gave him a hopeful smile as he approached the table. He did not return it. This meeting was just a formality. His mind was already made up, and the sooner he could get this over with and get back to Holly, the better.

"Thanks for coming," she said as he pulled out a chair and sat down across from her.

"You didn't give me much choice, Eve. I want this over with."

"We always have a choice, Adam," she said softly.

He ignored that. If she wanted to spend the next five minutes believing that he came here for any other reason than to get her out of his life once and for all, that was her issue. One drink and he was gone. That was the deal.

Eve poured them each a beer, then dropped a shot into each mug.

"Boilermaker?" Adam asked, raising a brow. "Not really your style, is it, Eve?"

She gave him an enigmatic smile. "If you're only giving me one drink, I thought it should be a good one."

He couldn't argue with that. Lifting the mug, he downed a quarter of it in one deep swallow. The beer was ice-cold and smooth; the whiskey, top-shelf. Under different circumstances, he would have appreciated it more.

"The meter's running, Eve. If you have something to say, you should get to it."

Her smile faltered for just a moment. "Fair enough. All right. Here it is: I love you, Adam." She paused expectantly, searching his face intently for a reaction. Exactly what she was waiting for, he hadn't a clue. Had she expected him to be moved by that? Or, God forbid, to return the sentiment?

Adam's expression didn't change when he finally said, "That's it?"

"That's enough, isn't it?" she asked. "I *love* you, Adam. I've never felt anything like this before."

He took another drink, reducing the amount remaining in the mug to half. "You don't love me, Eve. You only want what you can't have."

Her expression hardened slightly as she began to realize that her declaration of love was not having the desired effect. "How can you possibly know what I feel?"

"I don't." He shrugged. "But I do know what love is. It isn't flirting with and fucking every guy unfortunate enough to catch your attention."

Guilt suffused her features even as flames erupted in her eyes. "I didn't care about any of them! I was trying to make you jealous!"

Adam continued as if she hadn't spoken. "It isn't calling all hours of the day and night to check up on me."

Eve's voice began to rise, growing increasingly shrill. "You weren't calling me! And I missed you! Is it so bad that I wanted to hear your voice?"

"And it sure as hell isn't stalking and threatening every woman I talk to for more than five minutes."

"You are *mine*, Adam. I just wanted them to know that."

"Goddammit, Eve!" he said, pounding his fist on the table in frustration as the last of his hope for a clean and easy break faded away. "I am *not* yours! It was one fucking night!"

"It was beautiful—"

"It was *sex*. Nothing more, nothing less."

Eve shook her head vigorously in denial. "No. You love me. I felt it here"—she brought her hand to her heart—"when we made love."

"We did not make love. We had sex, sex that *you* initiated. I did not, nor will I ever, love you, Eve. I'm sorry."

For a brief moment, Eve looked like she was going to erupt. Adam prepared himself for the sting of her palm across his face. He wouldn't have stopped her. His words, however true, were cruel and meant to shock her into acceptance.

Then the hard lines in her face evened out, and her expression went oddly blank. "You're scared of commitment. I get that. I really do. It's why I've been so patient. But you can't keep seeing other women, Adam. It confuses things."

Eve started looking a little blurry. Adam blinked a few times to get her back into focus. She wasn't just crazy, he realized. She was fucking nuts. Coming here had been a complete waste of his time. It was obvious that nothing he said was going to make it through to her delusional mind.

He reached for his mug, tilting it up and guzzling the rest. He had kept his part of the bargain—one drink while he listened to what she had to say. Now it was time for her to keep hers.

Slamming it back down on the table decisively, he pushed away from the table and stood. A sudden wave of dizziness assaulted him, forcing him to grip the edge of the table so he wouldn't end up on his ass.

What the hell? He wasn't a big drinker, but one boilermaker shouldn't be affecting him this much, no matter how fast he drank it.

"Eve, you need help. Get some. I'm outta here."

He took one step, then two, before black dots started creeping in from the edges of his vision. His balance was totally off.

He stumbled, listing sideways and bumping into another table.

"Hey, Adam, you okay?" Paul called over.

Adam opened his mouth and said something. His tongue wasn't working properly, so it came out slurred and unintelligible.

"I told him he shouldn't have had that drink on top of his pain meds," he heard Eve say. She was right next to him, yet she sounded so far away. "Poor guy hurt his back and can't go an hour without agony."

What kind of bullshit was she spreading? He hadn't hurt his back.

Eve tried to put an arm around him to steady him, but he pushed her hand away.

"I don't think he should drive," said one of the regulars.

"Definitely not," agreed another, coming over to lend assistance. He slid himself under Adam's arm and guided him to a chair. "Easy there, Adam."

"Jackson?" Adam slurred, squinting at the big bald guy keeping him upright.

"That's right. I got you, man." The big guy called out to Paul from over his shoulder, "Better call his nephew."

"Don't bother," Eve said quickly. "I can take him home. Just help me get him into my car."

~ * ~

"Ma'am! Ma'am! Can you hear me?"

Holly moaned as the voice cut through the darkness. A man's voice. Definitely not one she recognized, and not the one she wanted to hear most. It wasn't Adam's voice.

She shifted and an intense wave of pain nearly sent her back into oblivion. She tried to breathe through it, but her throat protested, feeling raw and sore.

"Don't try to move, ma'am. Let us check you out first, okay?" Strong, warm hands pushed her back gently. *Not Adam's hands.*

She opened her eyelids, which seemed to have been coated with lead, to find warm brown eyes regarding her from beneath a shock of blond hair.

"What happened?" she mumbled. At least that was what she tried to say. Her lips felt swollen and cracked; her tongue, roughly the size of a cucumber; and the words didn't come out nearly as clear as they should have. "Who are you?"

"Jason Fielding, ma'am. I'm an EMT with the Covendale Fire and Rescue Squad."

Fire. That single word gave her mind the jump-start it needed, triggering her memories. The smoke alarm sounding, the vision of the gray and black tendrils seeping through the cracks in the old shed and curling around the eaves. She had run back into the house for her extinguisher, but she hadn't even gotten the door open before it exploded outward, sending both her and Max hurtling backward …

Max!

"Max!" she called out desperately, sending her into a coughing fit that had stars swimming behind her eyes. "Max! *Where's my dog?*"

Those strong hands kept her from moving too much. "Black and white husky? Freaky eyes?"

"Yes, yes, that's him. Have you seen him? Is he okay?"

"He's fine," the EMT said. His voice was commanding, yet deep and soothing. "One of the firefighters is checking him out. Smart dog. He's the one who led us to you. They'll bring him over in a minute, but you have to let me check you out first, okay?"

Thank God. Her breath came out in a whoosh of relief. Max was okay. She couldn't bear it if something had happened to him.

The acrid scent of smoke still hung in the air, burning her nose and throat with each breath. Turning her head to the side, she saw the smoldering remains of the small wooden shed. It and its contents were now reduced to nothing but a damp, charred pile of junk.

"Ma'am, look here, please." The guy with the kind brown eyes shined a tiny pen light into her eye.

She felt it clear through to the other side of her skull, as if he had just jammed a big knife right into the socket. She shut her eyes tightly and tried to wrench away, but he must have anticipated the move because he cupped her jaw with one of his hands and kept her from moving too far.

"I'm sorry about that," the man said, sounding like he really meant it. "I'll be as gentle as I can, all right?"

Holly nodded, the sharp pain down her back making her wish she hadn't done that. She tried to remain still and quiet while the EMT did his thing. He was only doing his job; it certainly wasn't his fault she was a major wuss when it came to handling pain.

He was quick and efficient, assessing her injuries with the skill of someone who had done this more than a few times. Despite his gentle touch, she couldn't help crying out when he hit upon some particularly tender parts.

While he worked, she tried to distract herself by thinking about something else. Right at the top of the list of Other Stuff to Think About was what the hell had just happened.

Things were still pretty fuzzy around the edges, but there had obviously been an explosion, and before that, a fire. But how? And why? Sure, she stored a couple of single-gallon gas containers in there for the mower and the weed-wacker and stuff, but like the equipment, they were practically brand new. She'd had to buy all that stuff when she got the cottage.

She stored a couple of rags in there, too, for checking the oil and whatnot, but so what? She kept the windows slightly cracked in the summer, and

the place was drafty enough to disperse any fumes
or vapors that might have built up.

Had something spontaneously ignited? It did
happen occasionally, though it was rare. Or maybe a
mouse or something had chewed into some wires?
There weren't any outlets in the shed, but a previous
owner had run a line to install a work light.

"Hey, Jason," said another, familiar-sounding
voice, pulling her back from her thoughts.
"Ambulance just pulled up. How is she—holy shit!
Holly, is that you?"

Holly forced her eyelids open again—they kept
shutting without conscious effort—and saw Adam's
nephew in full firefighter gear, sans face mask.
"Brandon?"

Damn, but the kid was good-looking, even
more so in his uniform. She wished she could have
snapped a picture for Liz. He had the makings of a
great romance novel cover model. *Maybe my next
hero should be a fireman,* she thought dizzily.

But wait, he was a waiter, wasn't he? And
going to school to be an engineer? What the hell
was he doing dressed as a fireman?

"I volunteer at the firehouse a couple hours a
week," he answered.

She realized she must have spoken her thoughts
aloud. Well, that explained the slight upturn of his
lips, even though his eyes looked worried.

"My dad was a volunteer fireman, and I took
all the training in high school so I could go out with

him on calls. You okay?"

No wonder Adam is so proud of the kid, she thought.

She nodded, more carefully this time, though she felt anything but okay. "Fucking awesome," she said, her brain too muddled and her body in too much pain to waste the effort on a filter. "Crap. I don't need to tip you for this, do I?"

He chuckled, though his handsome face still held genuine concern. "Jason's going to take good care of you, Holly. He's the best. Just listen to what he says, okay?"

"Okay," she breathed. It wasn't as if she had a choice. She could barely move without agonizing pain.

"Brandon, can you call Liz for me? Her number's in my cell, which should be in my pocket …" Holly tried to move her right hand, the only one that appeared to be working, across her body awkwardly to pull out her phone. Jason saw her struggling and helped her out, handing the phone to Brandon.

"Do I need to go to the hospital?" she asked, trying to focus on EMT Jason. He was still a little blurry around the edges. "Wow. You have amazing eyes. Very kind."

There was definitely going to be a fireman-slash-EMT in her next novel. She had read somewhere that firemen ranked number one on the list of female fantasies. How had she not yet tapped into that?

Jason smiled back at her with even, white teeth. "Thanks. And yes, you need to go to the hospital for some x-rays. The good news is, they'll be able to give you something for the pain there, too, once they know what you got going on."

"Oh, I got it going on," she mumbled, making him laugh.

Pain meds. That sounded *wonderful*. Holly was not a big fan of pain.

But she couldn't just leave.

"Someone needs to take care of Max …"

"I'll take good care of him, Holly," Brandon assured her. "You just take care of yourself, okay?"

"Okay …" Holly let her eyes close as they lifted her onto a stretcher.

Chapter Twenty-Five

With precise, careful movements, Holly gingerly got out of Liz's car. After hours of being poked, prodded, x-rayed, and MRI'd, all she wanted to do was crawl into her own bed and sleep for a week or so.

One broken arm, three cracked ribs, and a deeply bruised hip and shoulder hurt like hell. The pain meds they had given her at the hospital, only after they had determined she did not have a serious concussion, did help somewhat, but not nearly enough. The ER doctor had taken pity on her and written a prescription that should help with that. Holly wasted no time in downing two of the pills within seconds of picking them up at the drive-thru pharmacy on the way home. Already, a very welcome, pleasant numbness was beginning to seep into her limbs, muting her pounding headache from a ten down to a seven on the tolerance scale.

"You should have stayed overnight," Liz chastised, grabbing her overnight bag from the backseat and helping Holly into the house.

"I hate hospitals," Holly groused.

"Everybody hates hospitals, Holly."

"I want my own bed. I want Max." *I want Adam*, she added silently.

"I know," Liz exhaled, "but you're stuck with me tonight. Brandon texted about two hours ago. He said he'll bring Max over in the morning."

"Did he say anything else?" Holly asked, hoping she didn't sound as pathetic out loud as she did in her own head.

Given Brandon's involvement, she had half-expected Adam to show up at the hospital, or to find him waiting for her when Liz had brought her home. He hadn't shown. Granted, he hadn't said he would, but after last night, she had assumed they would be getting together, maybe picking up where they had left off this morning.

"No," Liz said quietly.

After seeing the look of sympathy in her eyes, Holly resolved not to ask again. *I am not going to be* that *girl*, she reminded herself.

It was just as well. She and Vicodin were going to be pretty tight for the next couple of hours, anyway.

Still, it would have been nice. Assuming he knew, that was. And why *wouldn't* he know? Brandon had been there on the scene and was watching Max, presumably at Adam's house.

"Okay then. Thanks for hanging out tonight, Liz. Sucks for you, though, huh?"

"Like I had anything better to do," Liz said, pulling off Holly's socks and shoes. Liz was trying to keep things light, but Holly could see the worry in her eyes.

Everyone should have a bestie like Liz, she decided. Someone to have her back. To be there when she found herself in the hospital and needed a ride home.

"And no offense," Liz continued, "but I'd rather be me than you right now."

"Yeah, me, too," Holly sighed, sinking into the pillow that still smelled like Adam. "Goodnight, Liz."

"Goodnight, Holly."

~ * ~

Sunlight streamed through the windows, searing his eyes. Adam rubbed at them, feeling as if he had been on one hell of a bender. It took him a couple minutes to get his bearings. He was in his bed, in his room, in his house, with absolutely no idea how he got there.

Adam dragged himself into the bathroom and caught a glimpse of himself in the mirror. He looked like shit. *What the hell happened last night?*

He gripped the edge of the sink, gritting his

teeth while willing the room to stop spinning. Adam didn't do shitfaced. Yeah, he tossed back a few with the guys sometimes, but he certainly hadn't been this out of it since he was a stupid kid. Like so many others, he had learned the hard way, but he *had* learned. He knew his limits, and he made sure he stayed well within them, especially with Brandon around.

He leaned over and splashed cold water on his face. *Fuck!* Why couldn't he remember anything? Most of his mind was focused on trying to stay upright and conscious, but to be this hung over, he should be able to recall something. Where had he been? Who had he been with? What had he done?

It was all a blur. There were vague, fleeting glimpses, but they couldn't possibly be right. They had to be nightmares because Adam wouldn't have willingly done *any* of those things.

He needed answers, and he wasn't going to find them in the porcelain a couple of inches from his nose. When he was relatively sure he could do so without face-planting on the floor, he pushed himself upright and took a deep breath. What he needed was caffeine and acetaminophen, preferably huge quantities of both. Then maybe he could get his shit together enough to figure this out.

It took one hand against the wall and all of his concentration to put one foot in front of the other, but he finally made it to the kitchen. Brandon was already there, sitting at the table. God bless the kid, he had made coffee.

Adam fixed himself a cup, sloshing more on the counter than he managed to get into his mug, then collapsed heavily into a chair. Even that brief foray from his bedroom to the kitchen had left him feeling drained and weak. His hand shook so badly he had trouble getting the mug to his mouth, which was probably just as well because the smell of the coffee brought the nausea back with a vengeance.

He closed his eyes, summoning every bit of self-control he had. He was *not* going to blow chunks like some teenager after his first bender.

Brandon looked up slowly and met his eyes. "Why did you do it, Uncle Adam?"

The look on the kid's face sent a wave of dread through Adam's unsettled stomach, but he steeled his emotions, needing information. His nephew obviously knew more than he did about what had gone down.

"Do what, exactly?"

Was that his voice? Either he was slurring his words or his brain wasn't translating the signals properly.

Brandon's next words had bile rising in the back of his throat.

"I thought you really liked Holly."

Holly! She couldn't have anything to do with this, could she? He was supposed to go over to her place last night. He had been looking forward to it all day. *Shit!* If he felt like this, what kind of shape was she in this morning?

But wait … That didn't make any sense. If he had made it over to her place, he wouldn't be *here*, and he wouldn't have woken up alone. Though, given the way his day had started, that was probably a good thing.

He clamped his eyes shut and scrubbed his face with his hands. *Remember!* he commanded himself. It was as though his brain was a blackboard and someone had just wiped it clean. All that remained were a few blurry white patches where the chalk had been.

While he couldn't recall any specifics, he knew in his gut that wherever he had been, whatever he had done, it hadn't been with Holly.

But *why* hadn't he been with Holly?

"I do care about Holly," Adam said, trying to remember where he had left his phone. He had to call her and … say what exactly? *Hi, Holly, it's Adam. Do you have any idea what I did last night? Why I'm here at my place, feeling like roadkill, instead of waking up in bliss beside you?*

He had finally found someone he wanted to be with, someone who had seemed just as happy to be with him. The last thing he needed was her questioning her choice to spend time with his sorry ass. Maybe his phone held some clue. He could at least look at the text and call log. Maybe that would trigger something to help him make some sense of this.

"You sure have a funny way of showing it."

The hair on the back of his neck rose and prickled, another wave of dread and cold sweat washing over him. Adam didn't know if it was purely physical, or a reaction to Brandon's words and the tone he had used. Despite their closeness, Brandon had never addressed him with such disrespect.

"Excuse me?"

"It just doesn't seem right. While Holly's laying in a hospital, you're out with your ex? Not cool, Uncle Adam."

Several things happened in quick succession. Adam's heart stopped beating for a couple seconds, then restarted by pounding painfully hard and fast against the walls of his chest. Then the contents of his stomach decided they didn't want to remain where they were, after all.

Adam barely made it to the bathroom in time. Then, after retching violently, his legs betrayed him and he ended up hanging on to the toilet to keep himself from face-planting into the tiled floor.

The next thing he knew, Brandon was leaning over him, pressing a cold, wet towel to a really sore spot on his temple. The disappointment on the kid's face was now mixed with genuine concern.

"Hang on, Uncle Adam. I'm going to call for an ambulance."

Adam grabbed Brandon's arm with surprising strength. "No ambulance," Adam said through clenched teeth as his body started to shake uncontrollably. "Tell me what happened."

Brandon blinked and studied his face. "You mean, you really don't remember?"

"Can't remember shit," Adam said, forcing himself to take deep breaths, knowing whatever it was, it was *bad*. "Just tell me what happened to Holly. Why is she in the hospital? Is she all right?"

For the first time, Brandon seemed uncertain. "Okay, but let's get you to the couch first."

Moving in any fashion was not in the least bit appealing, but Adam used every last ounce of willpower he had. With Brandon's help and a steel will not to vomit all over his favorite nephew, Adam managed to make it to the couch. By the time he got there, he was covered in sweat and feeling as weak as a pup. He sank down into the cushions and wiped his face with the cool cloth.

"Okay. Start talking."

"There was a fire at Holly's yesterday," Brandon began, taking the chair adjacent to the couch to remain close. "I was doing my volunteer shift down at the fire company when the call came in around three or so. Someone reported hearing an explosion and seeing smoke."

"Christ," Adam swore. "An *explosion*? You mean, like a gas leak or something?"

"Or something," Brandon said grimly. "It happened in one of the smaller outbuildings. A tool shed or something. The fire chief is working with the police. Nothing official yet, but the chief said it looked like a clear case of arson. He found evidence of an accelerant at the scene."

Adam knew just the building he was talking about; Holly had shown it to him when she had given him a tour of her place. It was situated to the left of the cottage, an old wooden structure in remarkably good condition, where Holly kept her gardening tools.

"The building was destroyed, but we got there in time to keep it from spreading to anything else."

"What about Holly? You said she was hurt. How bad? Did you see her?"

"Yeah, I saw her," Brandon said, his tone grave. "I've definitely seen her look better, but all in all, she was very lucky. She got banged up pretty good. Ended up with a couple of broken bones, cracked ribs, and a possible concussion, but it could have been a lot worse. A fire extinguisher was found not too far away from where she landed. She must have smelled the smoke and gone out to investigate. The chief thinks she was near the door when the place blew. The blast knocked her across the yard, but that was probably a good thing. It kept her away from the fire till we could get there."

"Jesus." Adam closed his eyes and tried not to picture it in his mind as his stomach twisted. "But she's okay?" He needed to hear it one more time. If anything happened to Holly …

"She'll live. The hospital wanted to keep her

overnight, but she signed herself out. Liz tried to talk her out of it, but Holly threatened to call a cab if Liz didn't give her a ride home."

Yeah, that sounds like Holly, Adam thought. "Liz is staying with her, I hope?"

Brandon nodded. "She was, until Holly's family started arriving this morning."

Adam frowned, remembering the little bit Holly had revealed about her family. She would probably appreciate Liz's company more.

"What about Max?" The dog was Holly's shadow, and if she had been affected, then he probably had been, too.

"Some singed fur, but none the worse for wear. Holly was really worried about him, though, so I told her I'd look out for him until she got back home. It was the only way she'd get in the ambulance."

"Max is here?"

"He was. I took him back first thing this morning. He was lost without Holly, and Liz said she needed him, too."

Adam sipped the cold water Brandon handed him. "And where was I during all this?" Adam finally asked, his voice quiet.

Brandon inhaled and exhaled deeply before replying. There was such pain on the kid's face that Adam knew he wasn't going to like the answer.

"I tried calling you to tell you what happened, but it went right to voicemail. When I got back from the firehouse, there was a message on the house machine from Paul up at the Lakeside Pub. He said he had to take your keys and that your truck was in the lot.

"Something didn't seem right," Brandon said, looking at his hands, "so I drove up there myself. Paul said you were in bad shape and that some chick gave you a ride home. After he described what she looked like, I knew who it was. What were you thinking, meeting up with Eve like that?"

Adam sighed and took a drink, his hand shaking enough that he had a hard time keeping it from sloshing over the sides. Some of the fog seemed to be receding and things were coming back to him little by little.

"I wasn't. Eve said she needed to talk to me. I said no, but she was persistent. She said, if I met her for one drink and heard her out, she'd leave me alone for good."

Brandon's eyes widened in disbelief. "And you *believed* her?"

"Not really. But she knew about Holly. I was afraid she'd start stalking Holly like she did the last woman I took out to dinner, and I didn't want to take the chance that it would have the same consequences."

"Holly wouldn't have given up so easily, Uncle Adam."

"I know. At least, I hoped I did. But I still didn't want Eve anywhere near her." He scrubbed his face with his hands. "I thought maybe I could prevent that from happening. I should have known better."

Brandon appeared to think about that, then nodded. "Okay. So, what happened then? After you got there, I mean."

"I don't know," Adam said, frustration heavy in the words. "I agreed to one drink, and that was all I had. Eve was spouting all kinds of crazy shit. I got up to leave, not feeling so good. Next thing I know, I'm waking up in my own bed, feeling like this. How did that happen, by the way?"

"After I talked to Paul, I called your phone again, hoping it wasn't too late to stop you from making a big mistake. Eve answered. She said you and her were back together. I demanded to talk to you, but she said you were in the shower and couldn't come to the phone."

Adam closed his eyes, coming to the sickening realization that those images he had thought were nightmares probably weren't.

"Then what?" he whispered with resignation.

Brandon looked down at his hands, unable to meet his uncle's gaze. "I didn't believe her. You seemed so happy lately, all because of Holly. After hearing you talk about Eve and how obsessive she was, I just couldn't see you leaving Holly and going back to her like that."

"I wouldn't," Adam agreed, glad that despite how things looked, the kid still had some faith in him.

"And with Holly in the hospital … well, I thought you should know about that, regardless. So, I drove over to Eve's place and pounded on the door until she finally opened it. She was in this skimpy robe thing, and you were as far gone as I'd ever seen you, practically passed out on her couch. You didn't even know who I was at first …"

Brandon closed his eyes and shook his head as if to dispel the image. "Anyway, I finally convinced you to come back with me. I got you to bed, and you went out like a light."

"Fuck," Adam breathed. How did things go from great to shit so quickly?

"Uncle Adam," Brandon said quietly after several long minutes. "Did you really only have one drink?"

"Yes!" Adam said, rubbing his face. "A boilermaker. One shot in a glass of beer. That's it."

"Did you order it yourself?"

"No, Eve had it waiting … for me …" His voice trailed off as the implication became clear. "She must have put something in it before I drank it."

Brandon nodded. "That's the only thing that makes sense at this point. Come on; we have to get you down to the clinic."

"What the hell for?"

"To have them draw your blood and do a tox screening."

"Later. I need to call Holly first."

Brandon's face took on that pained expression again. "Yeah, about that. Probably not a good idea right now."

"Why is that?"

"Because I'm pretty sure she hates you."

Chapter Twenty-Six

Holly closed her eyes and silently counted to ten as her mother and sisters prattled on. Relegated to the couch, she was bullied into remaining quiet and immobile while her immediate family swarmed around her in a frenzy of activity. The women of the McTierney clan cleaned, tidied, shopped, and cooked; the men inspected, repaired, mowed, and trimmed.

That was what they did when faced with adversity. They came together and took over, assuming complete and absolute control under the assumption that whichever family member was facing said adversity was incapable of doing so on his or her own. Holly supposed that some people might have taken comfort in that, but she was not one of them.

Her family meant well, but they were suffocating. It was one of the primary reasons Holly had moved away.

Another: the standard mumblings, spoken in quiet, hushed tones but overheard nonetheless. There were commentaries on the evils of single women living alone, away from their families, out in the middle of nowhere. There was a particularly long-winded discussion on the joys and inherent *rightness* of settling down with a man and having a family while one was still young enough to do so. And no family intervention would be complete without a thorough lecture on the benefits of having a *real* job, making *real* money and *real* benefits, while awaiting one's fated Prince Charming.

Prince. Fucking. Charming. Holly laughed out loud at that one, an incongruous cackle amongst the quiet mutterings of her much-loved but uninvited guests, drawing worried looks her way.

Holly caught her mother looking at the clock, no doubt wondering if it was time for her next dose of sleep-inducing narcotics.

She could have told her not to bother. Holly was counting the minutes, longing for the brief hour or two when she could slip back into a dreamless sleep and not think about … *him*.

For the hundredth time that day, Holly wished for the impossible. She wished her cell phone had been destroyed in the blast, or at the very least, run over and crushed by one of the fire trucks. She wished she hadn't been so eager to check her messages when she first awoke this morning. She wished she had stopped after the first one.

Most of all, she wished she had never met Adam Grayson.

Voice message #1: "*Holly, this is Adam. Listen, there's something I need to talk to you about. I'll explain everything tonight, but until then, just ... be careful, okay? Stay close to home and call me right away if anything weird happens. And Holly? Call me back as soon as you get this ...*"

It was a bit mysterious, that message, but nothing worrisome. Therefore, she had continued to voice message #2: "*Hi, Holly, Adam again. I planned on coming over right after work, but something's come up. I might be a little later than expected.*"

Also mysterious, but no big deal. Adam had a successful construction business. Sometimes things came up, like delayed deliveries, messed up shipments, scheduling conflicts, zoning delays. It was just the nature of the beast. Whatever it was, it must have been important.

At least, that was what she thought before she heard voice message #3. Though it had been left from Adam's mobile number, it was not his voice that time. No, voice message #3 had been left by Eve Sanderson.

"*Fun's over, Holly. Adam is back where he belongs ... with me.*"

And then there was the killer—voice message #4. The timestamp revealed that it had been left while she was waiting to be released from the hospital, and also from Eve: "*Adam knows where you are, and he doesn't care. He doesn't want to talk to you. Tell your bitch friend to stop calling already. You lost. Get over it and leave us alone.*"

If it had ended there, Holly might have been able to believe that there was some perfectly logical, rational explanation of how Eve had managed to get ahold of Adam's phone and leave those awful messages, especially since Liz had dropped some vague hints about how cunning and obsessive Eve could be when she set her sights on someone. Until she had a chance to talk to Adam and hear what he had to say, she was not going to fall prey to Eve's obvious attempts to incite trouble between them.

Which just went to show how love could turn a normally intelligent woman into a complete fucking idiot. Because, while she might be able to rationalize the voice messages, there was absolutely nothing that could explain the *pictures*.

At least half a dozen of them, all sent via text from Adam's phone. Selfies of Adam and Eve engaged in various sexual acts. Adam between Eve's thighs. Eve between his. Eve proudly straddling Adam's naked body.

It didn't appear as if Adam was aware the pictures had been taken. In the ones where his face was visible, his eyes were closed, his head thrown back as if in bliss. In contrast, Eve was smiling like the proverbial cat who had just eaten the canary in each and every one.

Maybe she was being naive, but Holly didn't want to believe that Adam knew the pictures had been taken. She *really* didn't want to believe that he knew and approved of Eve sexting them to her. In the end, it didn't matter. For whatever reason, Adam had hooked up with Eve. That was a bad enough scenario on the best of days, but knowing that it had happened while she had been lying in a hospital bed after being nearly roasted to extra-crispy was especially painful.

If there was anything good about the situation, it was that she had heard and seen those things before her family had started showing up. Thank God Liz had been there. *She* had gone ballistic.

Holly had felt sorry for Brandon when he brought Max back. Liz had set on him like a junkyard dog. To his credit, Brandon had seemed pretty sick about the whole thing, too.

"Hey, Holls," her younger brother David called, breaking her away from those morbid mental images as he walked through the front door like he owned the place. It hadn't taken him long to make himself at home. Of all her siblings, he was probably the one she got along with the best, but she was in such a crappy mood it didn't matter. It was a good thing he was also the most tolerant.

"Mail's here," he said, dropping down beside her on the couch. "This one looks important."

It was the little things like that that irked her the most. Not the fact that David walked out to the mailbox along the road and got her mail—that was a nice gesture—but the fact that he felt the need to paw through it and analyze each piece.

Out of principle, she leafed through each item, deliberately leaving the one he thought was important until the end. Immature, perhaps, but she was cranky and tired and sick with heartbreak.

The "important-looking" item was a legal-sized envelope stamped with the name Kline, Schweitzer, and Kline, a prestigious local law firm that catered to some of Covendale's elite. Holly removed the official-looking letterhead and read through the contents not once, but twice.

"Well?" David asked, leaning against the arm of the sofa.

"Fucking-A," Holly breathed. She handed him the letter and let him read it for himself.

The Covendale Valley Historical Society was trying to take her house away.

~ * ~

Adam couldn't remember ever feeling so sick, and it wasn't only because of whatever chemicals were still sloshing around in his system. Even with the rush put on it by his old friend and Chief of Police, Sam Brown, the results of the tox screening analysis would take several days to come back.

However, the nurse at the clinic who had drawn his blood had said his symptoms were consistent with the ingestion of some form of benzodiazepines, more commonly known as "date rape" drugs.

That was hard for Adam to accept. He had heard about those kinds of things before, but the news stories usually involved young, naive coeds, not thirty-two-year-old male contractors. According to the nurse, the reality was a lot different than the media-fueled perception.

Benzodiazepines were more prevalent than commonly believed, and went far beyond the Rohypnol, or "roofies," referenced and sometimes glamorized in Hollywood movies, she had told him. Surprisingly, some of the top names in prescription tranquilizers fell into that category.

While those mainstream drugs had legitimate uses and were often prescribed for things like anxiety or panic attacks, they were used illegally for recreational purposes, as well. When combined with alcohol, it was not uncommon for the user to experience anterograde amnesia—loss of memory while under the influence—dizziness, confusion, lack of coordination, and nausea, which pretty accurately described Adam's last twenty-four hours to a T.

He was drinking water by the gallon in an attempt to dilute and flush as much of the stuff out of his system as possible. With each passing hour, he was feeling more like himself. In another day or two, his physical malaise would be nothing but an unpleasant memory.

Too bad the *real* damage could not be so easily undone.

When Brandon had told him about the pictures, he didn't want to believe it. He knew Eve had some major issues, but that? It seemed surreal. Yet, he knew by the heavy, leaden feeling in his gut that it was not some horrible nightmare. Those vague images in his head, of things he hadn't wanted yet hadn't been able to stop, were all too real.

All it took was a look back in his phone's message log to see the proof. He had felt like throwing up again when he had seen those. There was nothing like looking at high-pixel, digital images of your half-naked ass engaged in various non-consensual sexual acts with a crazy, obsessed, psycho ex-lover.

As humiliating as it was for him, he couldn't even imagine how Holly must have felt. If he had seen pictures like that of her, he would have completely lost his shit.

God, she must fucking hate him. And he didn't blame her. He had been so stupid to think for one minute that Eve would step aside gracefully and let him get on with his life, but never in a million years would he have ever imagined she would go to those lengths.

He should never have agreed to meet with Eve. He should have followed his gut and gone right to

Holly's after work. He might not have been in time to stop her from getting hurt, but he would have been there for her. By her side. Holding her hand. Ensuring the EMTs and doctors were taking good care of her. And then he would have taken her home and watched over her. There would not have been any hurtful texts or photos, and she would have been safe and warm in his arms.

Instead, he was here, trying to flush God knew what out of his system, and Holly probably never wanted to see him again.

What was that saying? Hindsight is 20/20? Looking back now, it seemed all too easy to see the pattern of obsessive, borderline psychotic behavior. It was the stuff of Hollywood thrillers, and he'd had a starring role. Eve Sanderson needed some serious help.

Those mortifying pictures were now in the hands of the Covendale Police Department. Thankfully, his friend had assured him that the images would be kept private, unless absolutely necessary. Hopefully, that wouldn't happen.

After Adam had spent an hour or two in Sam's office with the door closed, the police chief had opened up an official criminal investigation. Not only had Eve's actions been morally reprehensible, but they were illegal.

Adam was confident the blood test would prove the existence of a foreign substance. He didn't do drugs; never had. There would be statements taken from character witnesses, interviews with his crew to show that he had been stone-cold sober before leaving work. But Sam had told him quite honestly that, while that might make him look good, it didn't prove he hadn't ingested the drugs willingly. Recreational drug abuse was not limited to punk teens and street addicts, especially when widely accepted, white collar stress-busters were involved.

He didn't like it, but that was the least of his worries. He was more concerned about Holly. As the level of Eve's obsession became increasingly clear, so did Adam's certainty that the recent series of unfortunate incidents surrounding Holly was not coincidental.

Sam's expression had grown progressively grim when Adam had expressed his concerns. The chief had been aware of the fire at Holly's, but the situation had taken on a whole new perspective when Adam had told him that Eve knew about, and was jealous of, his relationship with Holly. Adam had also told his friend about Holly's flat tires and Max's sudden unexpected sickness only a few days earlier.

Those were just the things he knew about. Holly wasn't the type to openly moan and complain when things went wrong. Had there been other things that she might not have mentioned?

Sam's advice made the situation even worse. "If all this came about because Eve was jealous of your relationship with Holly," he'd said, "then, for now at least, the best thing you can do is stay away from your girl. Until we can find something that will hold up in court, let Eve think her little plan worked and that Holly wants nothing more to do with you."

Adam didn't like it one bit. However, if it was the only way to keep Holly safe, he would do it.

Chapter Twenty-Seven

Holly's brother-in-law, Zach, a corporate lawyer based outside of Philadelphia, set the papers down and removed his reading glasses. "Civil suits aren't really my area of expertise," he said carefully, "but I have to call bullshit on this."

As annoying as her loud-mouthed, older sister Vicki was, Holly often wondered what the handsome, soft-spoken attorney had seen in her. Zach was nothing like Vicki. He was so laidback, always seeming to take everything her odd family threw at him in stride. Plus, he was one of the few who didn't seem to think Holly's life and career choices were causes for an intervention.

Holly was fond of Zach. Fond of all her sibling's spouses, as a matter of fact. It was only her blood relatives that she had problems with.

"It's all fluff and bluster," Zach continued as the rest of the family listened in.

The moment David had read the letter, he had called everyone in for a family meeting. Now there were McTierneys all over Holly's modest living room, standing, sitting, and leaning against every available surface. The space had never seemed quite so small.

"What exactly does that mean?" Holly's mother asked.

"It means, they don't have a legal leg to stand on. From what you've told me, Holly, this cottage and the land it sits on were divested from the original Penn estate a long time ago. It's been privately-owned and maintained for well over a century, and the Covendale Valley Historical Society has never felt the need to intervene before. I don't think there's any question that this is a personal attack on you. Who did you manage to piss off, anyway?"

It was impossible to take offense when Zach's eyes were filled with amusement and his mouth tilted up in that boyish half-grin. He knew about her fierce independent streak and, unlike the rest of her family, actually seemed to think it was a good thing, which pissed Vicki off to no end, so it was especially appealing.

"Swedish Barbie," Holly muttered, remembering Eve's thinly veiled threats that day.

"Excuse me?" That came from Vicki.

"She means Eve Sanderson," Liz said, breezing into the room with a bag of comfort goodies—ice cream, chocolate, and DVDs—for their planned two-person "fuck-the-world" fest later.

An FTW, as Holly and Liz called it, was a necessary response to a really big WTF moment in one of their lives. It was also a not-so-subtle hint for Holly's family to be on their way.

"Who?" Holly's younger sister Shelly asked, her head snapping up guiltily as she pretended she *wasn't* reading Holly's latest manuscript. Holly recognized the look immediately. It was the same look Shelly would get when they were teenagers and she had tried to sneak-read Holly's secret collection of romantic erotica.

When Holly narrowed her eyes in warning, Shelly's cheeks went pink, and if anyone was really listening, they would have heard the drawer of Holly's roll-top desk closing softly.

"Eve Sanderson. Holly's boyfriend's ex," Liz answered. Her mouth had grimaced as if saying the other woman's name left a bad taste in her mouth.

Several sets of eyes locked on Holly like heat-seeking missiles.

"Boyfriend?" Holly's mother said, her interest immediate and absolute due to that one, ill-chosen word.

Holly shot Liz a scathing glance as she squirmed under the pressure. She might just have to smack her BFF upside the head with that half-gallon of Rocky Road later, accompanied by repeated warnings to never, *ever* make any mention of male interest around her mother.

"He was just a guy I saw a couple times, Mom. No big deal." The lie burned on her lips, accompanied by an ache in her chest that was still too fresh, too deep. She forced it down, schooling her features into a mask of feigned indifference. She simply could not—*would* not—discuss Adam with her family, not yet. Maybe never.

"You didn't mention him."

"Because, like I just said, it was no big deal. We went out once or twice." *Most of the time, we stayed in and had wild hot monkey sex.* Holly almost let the words fly, just for the pure shock factor. It wasn't worth the inevitable fallout afterward, though.

"But—"

"Drop it, Mom," Holly warned sharply.

Eyes widened around the room while her mother openly gaped. Then, Colleen McTierney's eyes began to narrow, and *everyone* knew that mother and daughter were both gearing up for one of their epic battles.

"Right, then," Holly's dad said, standing before his wife could dig her heels in. "I think that's our cue. It's getting late and most of us have work in the morning."

Holly gave her father a look of grateful appreciation. Her father was a great, great man. And so wise.

"But Jack, Holly needs—"

"Peace and quiet," Jack McTierney finished firmly for his wife, his tone not allowing argument. "Liz is here to take care of anything else, right, Liz?" he asked, shooting a pointed glance Liz's way.

"Right, Mr. McTierney."

There were a few grumbles and protests as her father tried to round everyone up and out, but once Jack McTierney had made a decision, it was law. Everyone said their goodbyes and promised—i.e. *threatened*—to return the following weekend.

Holly gave a big sigh of relief when they were finally gone.

"God, they're exhausting," she said, closing her eyes and leaning her head back. Two days had felt more like two months. Now she remembered exactly why she had moved over an hour away.

"Yeah," Liz agreed, sinking down beside her with the tub of Rocky Road and two spoons. "But they mean well. Do you think, if I managed to hurt myself in a totally random and completely believable, un-staged freak accident, they'd come over to my place? I mean, jeez, Holly. I've never seen this house so clean. I swear there are enough pre-made meals in the freezer to last a month!"

"Yeah, there's that," Holly sighed. As much as it chafed to admit it, her family had been a tremendous help. Lord knew she hadn't felt up to running the vacuum, doing laundry, or cooking.

The downside was, Holly would probably

spend the next couple days putting things back where they belonged. Holly's mom's idea of organization was based on appearance; Holly's was based on accessibility and common sense.

A perfect example: her favorite zip-up hoodie was now hanging in the foyer closet instead of being draped across the kitchen chair where she could put it on when needed. Granted, her cottage had never looked so good, but Holly much preferred practicality over aesthetics.

Holly dug deep into the ice cream, relishing the total sensory experience. Ice cream was fucking awesome. Cold and rich and creamy, it never disappointed.

Unlike everything else in life.

"So ... Holly," Liz began slowly, drawing out the words, "we should talk."

The tone, the cadence, the phrasing—they were all clear indications that whatever Liz wanted to talk about, Holly was absolutely certain she *didn't*.

"Don't, Liz."

"Then don't talk, just listen. Because I'm only going to say this once, and then I am never, ever going to talk about it again."

Something in Liz's voice kept Holly from protesting again. "All right."

"I know you're hurting, and I totally get it. What Adam did was just awful. *But* ... maybe it wasn't completely his fault."

"Excuse me?" Holly said, stiffening. Liz was

her best friend. She was supposed to have her back, no matter what. No questions asked, just blind, one-hundred percent loyal support. "You're defending him now? You saw those pictures, Liz!"

"Yeah, I did," Liz admitted, biting her lower lip. "And didn't he, I don't know, seem kind of out of it to you?"

Holly *had* thought the same thing, but mostly because she had stupidly gone and fallen in love with the betraying bastard. It was her mind's innate self-defense mechanism kicking into gear, lessening the sting just enough to enable her to hang on to her last remaining shred of self-control.

"So, he got drunk first before he had sex with her. That makes it *so* much better."

Liz was quiet for a minute, staring into the ice cream as she swirled her spoon around the top. "I know I told you I didn't like Eve Sanderson, but I never told you why."

"I just figured it was because she was a spoiled, rich, self-centered, cunt of a whore bitch."

Liz's lips quirked a little at that, but her eyes were sad. "Well, there's that. But there is another reason, too."

Holly waited; she knew better than to rush Liz. Whatever she was going to say was obviously hard for her, and important. Liz wouldn't have brought it up otherwise.

"You know I have a younger brother, right?"

"Yeah. Nick, right? Moved out west

somewhere?"

"Wyoming," Liz confirmed.

"You don't talk about him much."

"No," Liz agreed. "But, at one time, we were really close. We're only about eighteen months apart in age, and we look enough alike that everyone always thought we were twins."

"What happened? Why did he leave?"

"Eve Sanderson." Liz spit out the name with more hate than Holly had ever heard coming from her lips. "I'll give you the Cliffs Notes version. She saw him at some party and decided she wanted him. At first, he was polite; told her he wasn't interested. Nick was crazy in love with his girlfriend, Annie, and was saving up money to get her a ring for Christmas."

Liz's voice quivered. She paused for a moment and took a breath. "Well, we know what happens when Eve doesn't get what she wants. She spiked his drink or, at least, that's what we think happened. One minute he was fine, the next, he was acting all loaded and out of control. I mean, don't get me wrong; Nick was no saint and could let loose with the best of them, but he always knew when to stop." She looked at Holly, who nodded mutely in understanding and encouragement.

"Anyway, one of his buddies saw what was happening and managed to get him into a bedroom to sleep it off. While Nick was passed out, Eve snuck in and texted Annie from his phone, pretending to be him. She said he'd drunk too much and needed a ride home. Annie was working second shift at the hospital that night. She was a nurse, which is why she wasn't at the party. She texted back, telling him to stay there and be safe, that she would be there for him as soon as her shift ended at eleven. When Annie showed up, she found Nick and Eve naked together in bed."

Holly's gasp sounded loud in the otherwise quiet room.

"Annie was devastated. She was every bit in love with Nick as he was with her. They were so good together, Holly. Perfect. The kind of soul-deep love you write about in your books, you know?"

Liz shook her head. When she spoke again, her voice was completely flat, devoid of emotion. "Annie ran out of the house and got back into her car. She got into an accident and was killed. Nick didn't find out until the next day when our dad tracked him back to Eve's to tell him."

"Oh, my God, Liz," Holly said, horrified. "That's awful!"

Liz had tears in her eyes, revealing and magnifying the soul-deep grief Holly had never glimpsed before. "Nick lost it. When he found out what happened, he snapped. He didn't remember any of it. Something broke in him, Holly. He left town after Annie's funeral and never looked back. He sends me cards, sometimes, but he refuses to talk to any of us. He says it brings back too many memories."

"I am so sorry, Liz." Holly reached down and pulled Liz into an embrace.

Liz accepted it for a few minutes, quietly sobbing against Holly's shoulder. Then she pushed away.

"So ... that's all I have to say," Liz said, sniffling and swiping at her eyes with the back of her hand. "You know what Eve is capable of now, so you can decide what you want to do with that information."

"Liz, I just don't know ..."

Liz held up her hand to cut her off. "No. No more talking. I meant what I said, Holly. Now grab that remote. I have half a dozen unrated movies, all with hot guys, and every one of them has at least one scene with full frontal nudity."

Chapter Twenty-Eight

Adam hung up the phone, feeling a fraction of the crushing weight on his chest begin to lift. It had taken a little over a month, but Eve Sanderson had just been formally arrested on a laundry list of charges, including arson, criminal mischief, and illegal use of a controlled substance, among others.

Sam said that the Sanderson's family lawyer had already posted bail and was pushing to have Eve remanded to a psychiatric facility for evaluation. From what Sam insinuated, it wouldn't be Eve's first time there.

Adam didn't really care where she went, as long as Eve was out of his life. As long as Holly was safe.

Holly. He hadn't spoken to her in weeks. At first, it had been because he was trying to protect her, but now ...

She hadn't made any attempt to contact him,

not that he had expected her to. He knew through Sam that she had cooperated fully with the investigation, and that she was recovering well from her physical injuries.

Adam rubbed absently at his chest. Thinking of Holly battered and bruised made him ache.

Beyond that most cursory information, he was lost. He had no idea what she was thinking, no idea how she felt. Did she hate him? Were her nights plagued with agonizing dreams of him as his were of her? It was inconceivable that she would ever be able to forget what had happened, but was there any chance she might someday be able to find it in her heart to forgive him?

The front door opened and closed, signaling Brandon's return from his shift at Applebee's.

Adam ran a hand down his face and tried to wipe away any trace of emotion before Brandon found him like that. He was a man, dammit. Men did *not* cry in front of other men.

Brandon paused briefly at the door, no doubt assessing the situation. It was a game they played. Adam pretended he was fine, and Brandon pretended to buy it.

"How was work? Okay?" Adam asked.

Brandon nodded, moving into the room. "Kind of slow now that the semester started up again," he said.

He went right to the fridge, grabbed the carton of milk, and poured himself a glass. The kid always did have a thing for milk, which might explain some of his sturdy six-two frame and perfect teeth. Brandon leaned casually against the counter, downed the entire glass, and then immediately poured another.

"Guess who came in for dinner tonight?" Brandon asked, his tone far too casual to be believable.

Adam swallowed hard. He had refrained from asking, but he did wonder every Tuesday night. Did Holly and Liz still go out every week? If they did, did they avoid Applebee's, knowing that Brandon worked there?

"How is she?" he heard himself asking.

"Different," Brandon answered vaguely.

"Different how?"

Brandon stared at him a long time before answering. "You know, maybe you should call her and find out for yourself."

Adam searched his nephew's face. The kid meant well, but … "Did she give any indication she would want me to?" he asked bluntly.

"No," Brandon admitted. "But—"

"Leave it, Brandon," Adam commanded firmly.

Before his nephew could say anything else, he turned on his heel and retreated into his bedroom, closing the door in a very clear message.

~ * ~

One day became the next, an endless cycle of days.

Holly couldn't seem to summon the energy to notice. Or care. She went through the motions, did what she had to do, but no more than that. She retreated into her own private world, preferring Max's company to anyone else's. The only exception was Liz, who continued to bully her into going out once a week. It was the only time Holly left the cottage, except for running occasional errands. Even those she tried to avoid, doing as much as possible online.

At least she didn't have to worry about losing her cottage anymore. She had received a letter the week after Eve's arrest to inform her that the Covendale Valley Historical Society "upon further reflection" had "opted not to pursue" acquisition of the property "at this time."

Eventually, summer turned into fall, Holly's favorite time of year. The air grew cooler, the days grew shorter. Each day she watched the leaves change colors a little more. Shades of green turned into brilliant hues of deep gold, orange, and crimson flame.

It was beautiful, yet she couldn't seem to wholly appreciate the wonder of it. It felt wrong. How could she take pleasure in so much vibrancy when she herself felt so barren inside?

Then the colored leaves were gone, too, leaving the trees bare and stark-looking. The brightly colored chrysanthemums and kale flourishing at the front of the house dried out; the last of the roses died and fell away; the variegated green and white blades of the abundant hostas withered away, leaving everything in varying shades of grays and browns.

It was as though the season had finally attuned itself to Holly's existence.

Too cold to sit outside, she sat at the kitchen table, Max splayed across the tops of her feet, lest she tried to sneak away while he napped. She sipped her coffee and stared blankly at the laptop screen. The cursor blinked patiently, incessantly, waiting for her fingers to tap on the keys and weave a new story, but it just wasn't happening.

At one time, writing had been her passion, the thing she loved to do above all else. In Holly's eyes, being an author was the best job in the world. With a few strokes of the keys, she could create entire worlds where true love existed, good triumphed over evil, and the endings were always happy ones. It had been her privilege to escape into those realms each and every day, some part of her believing that somewhere, someday, someone might read her stories and find a sliver of the same joy in reading them that she had in writing them.

But now ... it seemed pointless. To craft a good tale, an author had to be able to envision things like soul mates and happy endings, even if she no longer believed they were possible. These days, all her thoughts were dark. Her inner vixen, the one she used to call upon for sass and spice, remained silent and sullen. Even Vinny was forgotten, laying dormant in the bottom of her underwear drawer.

Despite all that, she missed writing. She longed to lose herself in a story, to let her fingers fly as her brain tried to translate those ideas and thoughts and feelings into written, readable prose. Where she could leave her own reality behind and create something better.

She needed that escape, but the ideas just wouldn't come.

Holly sighed and let her hands hover over the keyboard, twitching. Maybe, instead of writing about someone else's world, she should write about her own. If she couldn't create a new story, maybe she could find some measure of comfort in transcribing one she already knew.

And so, it began. Once Holly started, she couldn't stop. Everything she had held deep inside, everything she hadn't been able to talk about, came out on the pages. All the hurt, the ache, the tremendous feeling of loss and betrayal.

As she wrote, she began to realize it hadn't been *all* bad. There had been a lot of good crammed into those couple weeks. Sunset picnics on the lake. Pizza and movies. Incredible, mind-blowing sex.

The wonder of finding the one person you wanted to spend the rest of your life with.

Writing her own story became an obsession. It

was the first thing she did when she got up in the morning and the last thing she did before closing her eyes in exhaustion at night. She took breaks only when her body demanded it. The more she wrote, the more she remembered. All the little details that had gotten lost in the face of so much overwhelming drama. The feelings were so raw, so real, they translated onto the pages with minimal conscious effort.

It was beautiful and tragic and heartbreaking. It was *cathartic*.

Originally, Holly had begun writing it as a means of private, personal therapy. It was intended as an exercise to release some of the pain and begin healing. But by the time she finished, she knew it was quite possibly the best thing she had ever written.

Chapter Twenty-Nine

Adam was absolutely miserable. Winter had taken hold with a vengeance, which meant that many of his outside jobs had to be postponed. There was always inside work to be done, but in general, that kind of stuff required a lighter touch and a skilled hand. These last few months, Adam preferred the jobs that required less finesse and more brute force. He wanted to come home at the end of the day physically exhausted. The sooner he could fall asleep at night, the less time he had to think.

To regret.

Christmas was only two days away, and he just couldn't summon the urge to care. He hadn't even bothered to get a tree. There was no point. He would be spending the holiday alone this year, having declined his brother's repeated invitations.

Brandon had left three days earlier, so for the

first time in months, Adam didn't have to worry about putting up a front. For the next ten days, he could just *be*.

He poured out the chunky contents of the can of soup into a bowl, then popped it in the microwave to heat up. While he waited, he grabbed himself a beer from the fridge, as well as a package of rolls he had picked up at the mini-mart when he had gassed up on the way home.

When the microwave dinged, he took his dinner into the dark living room, not bothering to turn on the light. Pointing the remote at the flat-screen, he turned on the hockey game and settled in on the couch. With his feet planted on the coffee table, he raised the spoon to his lips, cursing when it burned his tongue.

He grabbed the cold beer and took a drink, swishing it around to relieve some of the pain. He had barely swallowed when the doorbell rang.

Adam cursed again. Who would be visiting him? Nobody he wanted to see, that was for sure.

He ignored it, expecting it to ring again. It didn't. A few moments later, he saw the brief swipe of headlights through the slight gap in the drapes.

Adam got up and went to the window, but he only caught the flash of taillights fading quickly as the vehicle drove away.

Odd.

Adam shrugged to himself and sat back down. He ate the rest of his meal without tasting it and watched the game without really seeing it.

Who had come to the door? Why had they only rung once? And why had they driven away like a bat out of hell only seconds after doing so?

Curiosity finally got the better of him. Adam set his empty bowl on the coffee table then went to the door. A blast of cold wind went right through his clothes, chilling him. Of course there was no one there; he didn't know why he had even bothered. Then his eyes landed on the package that had been left on the porch.

It was relatively small, wrapped in shiny white paper with glittering snowflakes and sporting a red satin bow. In crimson, calligraphic letters, a small tag bore his name.

He reached down and picked it up. It was heavy, like a book. Looking once more up and down the street and seeing no one, Adam took his package and went back inside.

He sat back down on the couch with the package in his lap, afraid to open it. In his heart, he knew what it was—a present from Holly. He ran his fingers over the paper for a while, thinking about how, only a short while ago, her fingers had probably touched this paper, too.

Adam then took a deep breath and gathered his courage. He carefully pulled at the tape along the folded seam until he could extract the plain white box within. Lifting the cover, he saw a manuscript. He drew in a breath when he saw the title: *Five*

Minute Man.

With shaking fingers, Adam removed the stack of paper from the box, turned to the first page, and began to read.

He read throughout the night, unable to put it down. He had never read anything Holly had written before, but was drawn in from the first page. She had a true gift, able to bring the characters to life, to paint a scene so clearly and thoroughly that he could picture it perfectly.

Of course, part of that might have been because he had lived it.

Hours later, eyes blurry, back aching from sitting for so long, Adam finally reached the last chapter and froze. It consisted of one page, blank, except for three handwritten words scrawled in Holly's flowing script:

To be determined...

The stone cottage was a vision. It looked like something out of a Thomas Kinkaid painting. Dusted with glittering snow, carriage lights glowed along the cobblestone pathway leading to the porch. Electric candle lights burned in every window; each sill was draped with boughs of evergreen tied together with big, red bows. In the large living room window, he could make out a Christmas tree, decorated with twinkling white lights and cascading white ribbons. Over the scent of fresh snow and wood smoke, he smelled the mouth-watering aroma of freshly baked cookies. Tollhouse, if he wasn't mistaken.

Adam fingered the small lump in his pocket and took a deep breath. Then he walked up to the door and knocked, careful not to dislodge the wreath of freshly cut pine that hung there.

As if she had been waiting for him, Holly opened the door almost instantly, wearing an oversized holiday-themed sweatshirt and slim fitting leggings that showcased the lovely curves of her legs. She looked smaller than he remembered, more fragile, but so much more beautiful. The light from within created a glowing nimbus around her head, making her look like an angel. The image took his breath away.

She tilted her head up, those big green eyes looking right into his with so much guarded hope he thought his heart might explode.

"Merry Christmas Eve, Holly," he said, his voice thick.

"Merry Christmas Eve, Adam," she said in that low, musical voice of hers. "Would you like to come in?"

"Yes, thanks," he said, stomping his feet to get the snow off before stepping inside. He was immediately met with a push of warm, soft fur against his hand. "Hey, Max," he said, indulging the dog with a rub.

"He missed you," Holly said softly.

"I missed him, too," Adam said, meaning it.

He then straightened and cleared his throat before reaching down into his pocket and extracting the contents. "You gave me a gift," he said, "so it seemed only fitting that I give you one in return."

Holly stared at the small package for several long seconds, but she made no move to take it. It wasn't fancy, just a crinkled sheet of white paper folded around a box. Looking at it now, Adam realized he had done a pretty shitty job of it. Hell, he wasn't good at that sort of thing on the best of days. He couldn't help it if his hands were shaking like crazy when he had wrapped it.

"Go on," he coaxed. "Take it."

"You didn't have to," she said, but she reached for it, anyway.

He took some small pleasure in the fact that her delicate hands were trembling a little, too. At least he wasn't the only one.

"Yeah, I did."

She carefully pulled away the tape, just as he had done, revealing a small, black velvet box. Her attention, however, was focused on the inside of the paper she had just unfolded.

The last chapter of the book she had left him.

He heard her sharp intake of breath as she read the words. He, of course, already knew what they said.

"*To be determined*" had been crossed off, and beneath it had been written "*And they lived happily ever after.*"

Tears welled in her eyes as she looked up at him.

"Open it," he commanded.

Holly did. She lifted the hinged lid of the little, black velvet box and gasped at the sight of a diamond engagement ring, flanked by stunning, smaller emeralds and set in a custom white gold setting.

"Marry me, Holly."

No flowery words, no romantic poetry, just a heartfelt request.

Some might have thought Adam was taking a gamble. After all, he and Holly had only spent a couple weeks together before spending the next several months apart under some very unpleasant circumstances.

He knew better.

There was not a doubt in his mind that this was exactly the way things were meant to be, because he had read her story. In her written word, he had seen her heart. Her pain. Her love. Her forgiveness. He knew the depth of her feelings were only rivaled by his own.

"*Yes …*" she whispered through the tears.

Adam released the breath he didn't realize he had been holding, and before she had a chance to change her mind, he slipped the ring onto her finger and crushed his mouth to hers.

She had said yes. He was never going to let her out of his arms again.

~ * ~

Oh, how she had missed this. Missed *him*.

It had all become clear to her when she had started writing her story. *Their* story. She loved him. Adam was the other half of her soul, and without him, she was miserable.

Once she allowed herself to accept that, everything else fell into place.

The last six months had been hell, but they had made her realize what was truly important. And as the details of what Eve had done and the extent of her illness had become known, Holly was ashamed she had not given Adam the benefit of the doubt. She had been so devastated, so ready to believe he had betrayed her, that she hadn't been able to look past her own heartbreak to see that he, too, had been hurt.

She would never make that mistake again.

Holly tugged off Adam's coat and blindly managed to hook it on the coat rack. The rest of his clothing did not fare quite as well.

Individual garments, both his and hers, were unceremoniously removed and dropped as Adam used his much larger body to push her farther into the house.

"I missed you," Adam told her, breaking away from her mouth, breathing every bit as heavily as she was.

"Less talking," she demanded, pulling him down onto the strategically placed nest of blankets on the floor in front of the fire. She didn't think he had noticed, consuming her as he was, but she was wrong.

"Expecting someone?" he growled, settling his heavy weight over her.

She was prevented from answering right away as he cupped her possessively between the legs while he used his mouth to create a trail of liquid fire beneath her jaw, down the column of her neck, finally latching *hard* onto her breast.

She needed him. Needed him so much. More than she had ever needed anyone or anything in her entire life.

"Hoping," she breathed, tangling her fingers in his hair and pulling him closer. "Praying. Wishing."

He grunted his approval, releasing one nipple with a loud pop before roughly taking the other. There was no slow seduction, nor did she want it. She wanted it rough, hard, and fast. She wanted her Five-Minute Man.

She felt him stroke her once, twice, before plunging his finger deep inside her. Her body arched up, offering itself to him if he would only just keep doing *that*.

Seconds later, she was gasping, already on the

precipice, when he replaced his skilled fingers with the blunt head of his turgid shaft.

"Yes!" she half-cried, half-screamed, needing him inside her more than she needed her next breath.

Adam obliged, plunging into her with one powerful thrust.

Her sex clenched around him greedily, starved for that which only he could provide.

"Holly!" he roared out above her. "Forget five minutes, baby. I'm not going to last five seconds ..."

Epilogue

Nine Months Later

Holly shifted in her chair again, trying to relieve some of the ache that had been plaguing her lower back for the last two hours. She smiled and greeted the seemingly unending stream of people lined up to get her to sign their books. Closing her eyes briefly, she tried to imagine Adam's strong hands massaging her and felt instantly better.

As of that morning, *Five Minute Man* had been among the top ten, most requested downloads on the major online retailers. The recent publicity had resulted in a surge of demands for her previously published books, as well. Holly declined nearly all the appearance requests she received on a daily basis now, but this was a special favor to the local bookstore that had been supporting her and showcasing her works all along.

"I loved this," confided one rosy-cheeked grandmother to Holly, her crystal blue eyes sparkling. Eyes that looked remarkably like her son's.

"Too bad it's not real," sighed a much younger, doe-eyed woman in line behind her.

"Oh, but it is," the older woman said emphatically before Holly could comment.

"Really?" the brunette asked doubtfully.

"Oh, yes. It was like that for me and my Charlie." She beamed, then turned to Holly. "And for you, too, wasn't it?"

"Yes," Holly confirmed, smiling back at her. Knowing that her mother-in-law had read their personal, and occasionally explicit, love story probably would have been more awkward if the woman wasn't such an open-minded, self-professed fan of Holly's work. The two had often chatted late into the night about possible plots and themes and alpha males, while Adam and his father puttered around the cottage. The fact that Adam's mother was here now, when Holly's own mother was too embarrassed to do the same, warmed her heart.

Of course, some of that might have to do with the fact that Holly was already three days past her due date and Adam had enlisted his entire family's assistance to ensure she was never out of their sight. He was so protective that way, and Holly loved him for it.

"Wow. You are so lucky."

"Yes," Holly agreed, rubbing her distended belly as the first real labor pain hit. "Yes, I am."

Pssst...Want to know more about Adam and Holly's wedding? Check out Liz's story in **All Night Woman**, *Book 2 of the Covendale Series...*

Author's Note

You know, it's funny where the seed for a story originates sometimes. In my case, I never know where my next idea will come from. Sometimes it starts as a dream; other times, I hear a song and the lyrics create an alternate reality. In the case of *Five Minute Man*, the impetus was a phrase on the Urban Dictionary website: *ass-tag convention*. It was the word of the day on September 21, 2013.

So, how did something as innocuous as the "*ass-tag convention*" become a story? Well, it's just one of those things that stuck in my head. First, I wondered what, if any, harm I was bringing to my family by being one of those women who tends to cut the tags off things. I mean, it's impossible to have an ass-tag convention if there's no tag, right?

Then I began to wonder who would actively employ the ass-tag convention. Male or female? Young or old? Someone concerned with hygiene, obviously. Someone not overly touchy-feely, who likes to set definitive personal limits.

A character started to form in my mind, a woman, past youthful ambivalence chronologically and on the cusp of middle-age mentally. Adorably prickly, but soft at heart. Pretty and natural, but not beautiful. A woman who, through both nature and nurture, preferred to distance herself from the world, to create and be content with her own little bubble of existence.

As with all my stories, I added in a few snippets from my own life. My love of animals, and my profound belief that almost any dog is worth a dozen humans. Regular GNOs with my BFF to keep me sane and talk about things that no respectable wife or mother should probably talk about over under-550-calorie menus and unsweetened iced teas. A love of reading and writing romantic and erotic fiction that provides an escape, allows me to lose myself in alternate worlds cruelly hinted at by professional taunters like Walt Disney and goddesses like Lora Leigh and Sherrilyn Kenyon.

(I just want to add here that I have met both of these amazing ladies, and I am even more of a fan now than I was when I first started writing.)

Which is where the whole five-minute man thing came in.

Fantasy? Sure. But we all need something to believe in. When we outgrow Santa Claus and the Tooth Fairy, when we realize the hot guy in the famous boy band is NOT going to spot us back in the hundred and seventeenth row and profess his true love, when we get out on our own and realize that men are not the perfect creatures we've always dreamed of, we find ourselves looking for that next thing we can close our eyes and fantasize about.

Like Holly, when I write, I create a world I'd

like to live in, with people I'd like to hang out with. When I read my favorite authors, I enter their worlds. Their works are my mind's vacation from real life, from laundry and dishes and scrubbing bathrooms and worrying over ass-tag conventions and the long-term psychological damage I'm inflicting on my kids without realizing it. Their stories give me a place to go, something to think about, when I'm waiting or driving or doing any of the thousand things wives and mothers are supposed to do.

Hopefully, reading *Five Minute Man* was a little mini-vacay for you, too.

Thanks for reading Adam and Holly's story

You didn't have to pick this book, but you did. Thank you!
If you liked this story, then please consider posting a review online! It's really easy, only takes a few minutes, and makes a huge difference to independent authors who don't have the mega-budgets of the big-time publishers behind them.

Do you like free books? How about gift cards?

Sign up for my newsletter today! You'll not only get advance notice of new releases, sales, giveaways, contests, fun facts, and other great things each month, you'll also get a free book just for signing up ***and*** be automatically entered for a chance to win a gift card every month, simply for reading it!

Get started today!
https://abbiezandersromance.com/newsletter-signup/

Also by Abbie Zanders

Contemporary Romance – Callaghan Brothers

Plan your visit to Pine Ridge, Pennsylvania and fall in love with the Callaghans

- 📖 Dangerous Secrets
- 📖 First and Only
- 📖 House Calls
- 📖 Seeking Vengeance
- 📖 Guardian Angel
- 📖 Beyond Affection
- 📖 Having Faith
- 📖 Bottom Line
- 📖 Forever Mine
- 📖 Two of a Kind
- 📖 Not Quite Broken

Contemporary Romance – Connelly Cousins

Drive across the river to Birch Falls and spend some time with the Connelly Cousins

- 📖 Celina
- 📖 Jamie
- 📖 Johnny
- 📖 Michael

Contemporary Romance – Covendale Series

If you like humor and snark in your romance, add a stop in Covendale

- 📖 Five Minute Man
- 📖 All Night Woman
- 📖 Seizing Mack

More Contemporary Romance

- 📖 The Realist
- 📖 Celestial Desire
- 📖 Letting Go
- 📖 Protecting Sam

Cerasino Family Novellas

Short, sweet romance to put a smile on your face

- 📖 Just For Me
- 📖 Just For Him

Time Travel Romance

Travel between present day NYC and 15th century Scotland in these stand-alone but related titles

📖 Maiden in Manhattan
📖 Raising Hell in the Highlands
(also available as a box set)

Paranormal Romance – Mythic Series

Welcome to Mythic, an idyllic communities all kinds of Extraordinaries call home.

📖 Faerie Godmother
📖 Fallen Angel
📖 The Oracle at Mythic
📖 Wolf Out of Water

More Paranormal Romance

📖 Vampire, Unaware
📖 Black Wolfe's Mate (written as Avelyn McCrae)
📖 Going Nowhere
📖 The Jewel
📖 Close Encounters of the Sexy Kind
📖 Rock Hard
📖 Immortal Dreams

📖 Rehabbing the Beast (written as Avelyn McCrae)

Howls Romance

Classic romance with a furry twist

📖 Falling for the Werewolf
📖 A Very Beary Christmas

Historical/Medieval Romance

📖 A Warrior's Heart (written as Avelyn McCrae)

About the Author

Abbie Zanders loves to read and write romance in all forms; she is quite obsessive, really. Her ultimate fantasy is to spend all of her free time doing both, preferably in a secluded mountain cabin overlooking a pristine lake, though a private beach on a lush tropical island works, too. Sharing her work with others of similar mind is a dream come true. She promises her readers two things: no cliffhangers, and there will always be a happy ending. Beyond that, you never know…

Made in the USA
Coppell, TX
15 June 2022